Paul Drake entered the restaurant carrying a small object wrapped in newspaper. He put the package on Perry Mason's table and from it came a faint but unmistakable sound of steady ticking.

"The buried clock?" Mason asked. "Where did you get it?"

"We found it about ten feet from the place where it was concealed the first time. And if it means anything to you, that clock is two hours and forty-five minutes fast."

Mason took out a piece of paper and did some rapid figuring. "That puts it almost exactly on sidereal time, Paul."

"Why the devil would a man want a clock that keeps time with the stars?"

"That, my boy," said Mason, grinning, is a question we'll dump in the lap of the D.A.!"

THE CASE OF THE BURIED CLOCK
was originally published by
William Morrow & Company, Inc.

THE CASE OF THE
BURIED CLOCK
ERLE STANLEY GARDNER

PUBLISHED BY POCKET BOOKS NEW YORK

THE CASE OF THE BURIED CLOCK

William Morrow edition published May, 1943

A *Pocket Book* edition
1st printing........January, 1950
14th printing......December, 1969

This *Pocket Book* edition includes every word
contained in the original, higher-priced edition. It is printed
from brand-new plates made from completely reset, clear, easy-to-read
type. *Pocket Book* editions are published by Pocket Books, a division
of Simon & Schuster, Inc., 630 Fifth Avenue, New York, N.Y. 10020.
Trademarks registered in the United States and other countries.

L

CAST OF CHARACTERS

CAST OF CHARACTERS

THE CASE OF THE
BURIED CLOCK

1

The coupe purred up the winding highway. Adele Blane's dark eyes, usually so expressive, were now held in a hard focus of intense concentration as she guided the car around the curves. She was twenty-five, but, as her sister Milicent had once said, "Adele *never* looks her age. She either looks five years younger, or twenty years older."

At her side, Harley Raymand held the door handle, so that swaying around the curves wouldn't swing his weight over against his left elbow. The Army surgeons had managed to fix up the joint. "It'll be stiff for a while," they had told him, "and it'll hurt. Try and work that stiffness out. Keep from jarring it as much as you can."

A few hundred feet below the car, jumping from foam-flecked rocks to dark, cool pools, a mountain stream churned over boulders, laughed back the sunlight in sparkling reflections, filled the canyon with the sound of tumbling water.

The road crossed the mountain torrent on a suspension bridge, started a slanting climb up the other side of the canyon, mounted at length to a pine-clad plateau.

Off to the left, the Southern California sunlight turned the towering granite mountains into a dazzling brilliance which made the shadows below seem as blotches of ink. The road wound along a plateau region where pine trees oozed scent into the warm dry air. Far off to the right, the heat-haze which enveloped the lowlands looked like molten brass whipped up to a creamy consistency and poured into the valley.

"Tired?" Harley Raymand asked Adele.

"No—a little worried, that's all."

She negotiated a sharp turn, concentrating on the road. Then, on a brief straightaway, flashed him a glance. "I'll bet *you're* tired," she said suddenly. "Almost your first day home, and I drag you up here to Dad's cabin. . . . And you had your talk at the luncheon club, too."

Harley said quietly, "No, I'm not tired. . . . I'd just forgotten there were places like this, and now I'm getting reacquainted with them."

"Didn't your talk at the luncheon club tire you?"

"Not me," he laughed, "only the audience."

"Harley, you know I didn't mean it that way."

"I know."

"What did you tell them?"

"I guess they expected the usual flag-waving. I didn't give it to them. I told them this time war was a business —and they'd have to work at it just as they worked at their businesses, without fanfare and bands and hulla-baloo. And I told them we'd get licked if we *didn't* work at it."

Adele Blane said suddenly, "Harley, are you going to work for Father?"

"He telephoned me to drop in and see him when I had a little time and knew what I wanted to do."

"He needs someone like you, someone he can trust . . . not like— Oh well."

"Jack Hardisty, eh? Didn't that turn out all right, Adele?"

"Let's not talk about it," she said shortly. Then, apologizing for her shortness, "No, it definitely didn't turn out all right, but I'd rather not discuss it."

"Okay."

She flashed him a quick glance. The indifference in his

2

voice was new to her. In many ways this man was a stranger. A year ago she had known his every mood. Now he could surprise her. It was as though the Kenvale world were being viewed in his mind through the wrong end of a telescope, as though things which loomed important in her mind seemed merely trivial in his.

The road entered another steep canyon, climbing sharply. At the summit of this grade Adele turned sharply to the left, ran up a grade to a plateau where the cabin, nestling at the apex of a triangular slope, looked as though it had grown there as naturally as the pine trees.

It was one story, with a wide porch running across the front and one side. The rail of the porch and the pillars were of small logs from which the bark had been removed. The outside was of shakes, and the weather had aged them until the cabin blended into the green of the background and the brown pine needles of the foreground.

"Look natural?" she asked him.

He nodded.

For a moment she thought he was bored, then she caught sight of his eyes.

"I've thought about this place a lot," he said. "It represents something that's hard to find these days—tranquillity. . . . How long will we be up here?"

"Not long."

"Can I help?"

"No, it's just a checking up, looking over the canned goods, seeing what needs to be done. You stay out in the sunshine and rest."

She watched him get out of the car, saving his left elbow. "You know your way around," she said. "There'll be some cold water in the spring."

She hurried on into the cabin, opening windows, airing the place out. Harley walked around the trail to the deep shadows where crystal-clear, cold water trickled

3

out of the spring. He used the graniteware cup to take a deep drink, then strolled out to a patch of sunlight beside a flat rock. His view took in the long slope across the deep canyon, now beginning to fill with purple shadows. There wasn't enough wind to start the faintest murmur in the tops of the pines. The sky was cloudless blue. The mountains rolled in undulating pastels except where jagged crags ripped their way into glittering pinnacles.

Harley propped his head back against a pine-needle cushion, half closed his eyes, experiencing that sudden fatigue which comes to men whose reserve strength has been sapped by wounds. He felt as though the effort of moving even an arm would require a superhuman expenditure of energy.

"Tick-tick-tick-tick-tick-tick-tick-tick."

Harley opened his eyes. A fleeting expression of annoyance crossed his face. He wanted so much to have utter silence, for just a few moments . . .

"Tick-tick-tick-tick-tick-tick-tick-tick."

Surely his watch couldn't be making that much noise. The thing seemed to be coming from the ground right by his ear.

He shifted his position and folded his coat into a pillow. The sound of the ticking was no longer audible. He was lying flat now, looking up at the lacework of pine branches traced against the blue sky. He was completely, utterly weary, wanting only to lie there, as though he were a pine needle which had drifted down to the ground to soak up oblivion.

He wakened with a start, opened his eyes, caught the lines of a shapely ankle and leg, the hem of a sport skirt.

Adele Blane, sitting on the rock beside him, smiled down at him with that tenderness which women have for men who are recuperating from wounds received in combat. "Feel better?"

4

"Heavens, yes. What time is it?"

"Around four."

"Gosh, I must have been asleep for a couple of hours."

"Not much over an hour, I guess. Did you go to sleep right after I left you?"

"Yes. I—I felt as though someone had pulled a plug in my feet and let all my vitality run out."

They both laughed. "And you're feeling better now?"

"Like a million dollars! That nap brought back my strength. . . . Ready to start back?"

"Uh huh, if you are."

He raised himself to a sitting position, shook out the coat, asked, "What's the clockwork mechanism for, Adele?"

"What clockwork mechanism?"

"I don't know. It probably regulates something. You can hear it over at the corner of the rock. That's why I moved."

He caught the significance of her glance and laughed outright. "Do you really think I have spells of delirium?"

She joined his laughter at once, but her laughter lacked spontaneity.

Slightly irritated, Harley said, "You can hear it for yourself, over at that corner of the rock."

She bent down, more as a courtesy than out of curiosity, quite evidently expecting to hear nothing.

He was watching her face when her detachment gave way to a sudden flare of puzzled bewilderment.

"That's what I meant," Harley said with dignity.

"It sounds—Harley, it sounds like a clock! It *is* a clock! It's right here!"

He scooped away the pine needles, clearing a small section of earth, and disclosed the lid of a lacquered tin box which had been buried with great care in the soil. He raised the lid.

5

Within the box, held securely upright by wooden blocks, a small-sized alarm clock was ticking steadily. It was, Harley saw, a clock made by one of the best-known manufacturers. Aside from the peculiar bracing, there seemed to be nothing unusual in its appearance. There were two small holes in the lacquered box.

Harley consulted his watch. "It's exactly twenty-five minutes slow. You wouldn't think it would be *that* far off. It's a good grade of clock. Notice this lid. It's almost flush with the ground. Just a few pine needles and a little moss have been placed over it."

"What a strange way to bury a clock!" Adele exclaimed.

Raymand laughed. "I don't know just what *is* the standard of normal in clock-burying. Personally, it's the first time I've ever heard of a buried clock. Are we—"

The sound of an automobile engine reached their ears, the motor of a car that was climbing rapidly.

Harley listened, said, "Sounds to me as though they're taking the road up here. Let's just drop the clock back into the box, put the pine needles over it, and stroll up toward the cabin. Perhaps whoever is coming in that car will—"

"Go ahead," she said. "You'll have to hurry."

Harley dropped the lid back on the box, deftly replaced the pine needles and little fragments of moss. "All ready," he said, taking Adele's arm.

Momentarily a clump of brush masked them as a car swung around the curve in the roadway to emerge on the little plateau. For a moment it was merely an indistinct object moving through the afternoon shadows cast by the trees. Then, as it debouched into a sun-flecked opening, it resolved itself into a two-tone blue coupe.

"It's Jack Hardisty's car!" Adele exclaimed.

Abruptly the car came to a stop. The door opened.

Jack Hardisty scrambled out to the needle-carpeted clearing.

Adele Blane's hand rested on Harley's arm as he started to move out from behind the brush. *"Don't!* Wait here, *please!"*

They stood motionless, watching Hardisty reach into the interior of the car, pull out a long-bladed garden spade, and start toward the outcropping of rock. Then he stopped abruptly as he saw the indistinct figures behind the brush.

For a moment the pair were gripped in that rigid immobility that comes with discovery. Then they broke into the stiff action pattern of those who are trying consciously to act naturally—and making a dismal failure of it.

"Walk out from behind the brush as though we hadn't seen him," Adele coached in a low voice.

Harley Raymand felt the pressure of her hand on his arm. They moved awkwardly from behind the brush into the patch of afternoon sunlight. From the corner of his eye, Harley saw Jack Hardisty hastily push the spade back into the car. Adele, now in plain sight, registered a surprise which, to Harley's self-conscious embarrassment, seemed as obvious as the overdone pantomime acting of the silent screen.

"Why, there's a car—it's Jack!"

She had raised her voice so it would carry, and her attempt at surprise left Harley with no alternative save to follow suit.

Hardisty came walking toward them.

He was narrow across the shoulders, pinched in the face, but his double-breasted gray suit had the unwrinkled neatness which is found only in the clothes worn by thin men whose pores exude a minimum of body moisture. His nose was prominent, high-bridged, and supported bowless glasses.

7

"Well, *well!*" he exclaimed. "It's our hero returned from the wars! How *are* you, Harley? Hello, Adele."

The hearty, man-to-man enthusiasm of Jack Hardisty was overdone. He hadn't the capacity of lusty emotions, and his attempt to put punch into his greeting was so synthetic it carried its own stigma of insincerity.

Harley Raymand couldn't bring himself to respond to Hardisty's vociferous cordiality. Adele Blane held herself aloof, and the first rush of sentences stagnated into a slow-flowing trickle of conversation.

"Well," Hardisty said, "I want to get on up to the cabin. Lost my favorite knife when I was up here a week ago. . . . Thought I might have left it out around the grounds, or perhaps it dropped down behind the cushions in that big chair."

"A week ago," Adele said musingly. "Why, I didn't think anyone had been up here for ages. The cabin didn't look as though it had even been opened."

"Oh, I didn't straighten it up any, just ran up for a few hours' rest. . . . Like to get away from the noises and the blare of radios. It's peaceful up here, helps you reach a decision when—"

He became abruptly silent.

Adele said with dignity, "We were just leaving. I was looking the place over. Dad is coming up tomorrow night. Are you ready, Harley?"

He nodded.

"Hope you find your knife," Harley said politely, as they started toward the place where Adele had left her car.

Hardisty became instantly effusive. "Thanks, old man! Thanks a lot! Hope that arm doesn't give you any trouble. Take care of yourself. Don't try to do everything all at once. Take it easy, boy. Take it easy."

It was not until after they had reached the foot of the grade and were on the straight stretch leading to Kenvale, that Adele suddenly gave vent to her feelings. "I *hate* him," she said.

"He'd do a lot better if he acted naturally," Harley agreed. "Someone's sold him on the idea of impressing people with his personality. He just hasn't that kind of a personality. It's as though a dummy tried to do a strip tease."

"It isn't that," she said. "I can stand that stuff, because I think he has an inferiority complex; but it's what he's done to Father."

Harley started to ask a question then thought better of it.

Adele said, "He's short over ten thousand dollars at his bank. You know as well as I do, it was Dad's money and Dad's influence that got him in over there."

"I'm afraid I'm a little out of touch with things," Harley apologized.

"Dad started a bank in Roxbury, made a six-thousand-dollar-a-year job for Jack—just because he was Milicent's husband."

Harley remained silent.

"Jack Hardisty," Adele went on, "has been reading books on salesmanship and on influencing people. He hides his half-starved, whimpering soul behind the mask of a big, bluff, backslapping paragon of pep. . . . It's all I can do to keep my hands off of him."

"The shortage known?" Harley asked.

"Only the bank directors and the bonding company. Dad had guaranteed the bonding company against loss on Jack's policy. They didn't want to write it—something in Jack's past. I suppose Dad's got to make it good and hush it up and—I shouldn't have shot off steam about this, Harley. Forget it, will you?"

Harley smiled at her. "It's forgotten."

She realized that a year ago this would have absorbed his thoughts and dominated their conversation. Now he apparently dismissed it from his mind as a minor matter. She said, "That's why Dad needs someone he can *trust.*"

He might not have heard her, or hearing, might not have realized the implications to himself. He merely asked, "Why did Jack bury that clock up at the cabin?"

"Do you think he did?"

"He certainly was starting over toward that granite outcropping, and he'd taken a shovel from the car."

She said, "I've been trying to think that out. I can't understand it. I—why, here comes Milicent's car! She—"

Adele broke off talking, to wave frantically at an approaching light convertible. The car slowed to a stop. Milicent Blane's eyes regarded them from behind neat-fitting, rimless spectacles. Impatient with the life of idleness which was open to her as the daughter of Vincent Blane, she had studied to become a registered nurse. Her marriage had interrupted her career, filling her at first with a radiant happiness which had withered almost as it bloomed. Her face, never very expressive, had become a mask of grave immobility.

"Hello! Been up to the cabin? Why, hello, *Harley!* I didn't recognize you for a minute! Well, *how* are you?"

Harley Raymand opened the door of Adele's car, walked around to shake hands with Milicent.

"It certainly *is* good to see you. They told us you were pretty well shot up. . . . Are you feeling all right now?"

"Tough as taxes. I'm glad to see you again."

She turned to Adele. "Been up to the cabin?"

Adele nodded.

"Did you—I mean—was . . . ?"

"Yes," Adele interrupted, reading her thoughts. "He came up just as we were leaving."

Milicent's attempt to be courteous, to show a polite interest in Harley's return yet get started for the cabin

10

without so much as a minute's delay, made her rather confused.

"Well, it's nice to have seen you," she said, slipping the car into gear and holding out the clutch. "I hope we'll be seeing you. Hope you see us—I mean I hope you'll—oh, we'll get together."

Her foot slid back. The car lurched ahead.

Adele watched her dubiously for a few moments, then started on toward Kenvale. "The rat," she muttered savagely under her breath, "isn't good enough to be her doormat."

"She knows about what's happened?"

"I don't think so. I certainly hope not."

"Then why was she in such a dither to locate her husband?" Harley asked.

"Because there are—domestic troubles, too. Let's not talk about Jack. . . . Where are you staying, Harley?"

"At the hotel."

Adele's foot pushed down on the throttle. After the tire-conserving pace at which she had been operating the car, the new speed seemed terrific, although the speedometer showed it as only fifty-five miles an hour.

She laughed apologetically. "I just thought of an appointment I had. I'm going to be late. . . . That's the trouble with you, Harley: you make me forget things. And here it is almost sunset."

Harley Raymand showered, stretched out on the bed, and almost instantly sank into exhausted lethargy. The speech at the luncheon club, his trip to the cabin, had used up energy, and he was being forced to a realization that his available store of energy was limited. Those bullets had sapped more of his strength than he had thought possible.

The telephone rang sharply, and the convulsive start with which he regained wakefulness made him realize just how nervous he was. He switched on the lights, answered the phone.

The voice of the switchboard operator advised him that a Mr. Vincent P. Blane was waiting in the lobby.

"Blane!" Harley repeated, in surprise. "Tell him— Tell him I'm dressing. It'll be ten minutes before I can join him in the lobby. If he's in a hurry, he can come on up here."

Harley dropped the receiver into place, put on his shirt and trousers, and was just putting on his shoes when he heard Blane's knock at the door.

It had been but little more than a year since Harley had last seen Adele's father, yet he was shocked at the change in the man. Definitely, he was older, more worried. There was still the same charm of manner—that courteous interest in others which was neither effusive on the one hand, nor patronizing on the other, but had the graciousness of dignity about it.

Harley knew that Blane's errand was important, could

see that he was under a great strain, yet the man wouldn't think of mentioning his problem until after he had done those things which were demanded by courtesy: an apology for his intrusion, a solicitous inquiry after Harley's health.

"I'm sorry," Blane began, "if I wakened—"

"It's all right," Harley interposed, trying to make things easier. "I'm just a little lazy these days. Was there something I could do for you, Mr. Blane?"

Under the bushy eyebrows, Blane's keen gray eyes showed gratitude. "Mighty nice of you to make such a suggestion, Harley. . . . As a matter of fact I'm a little worried about Adele."

"What about her?"

"You were with her this afternoon?"

"Yes. We went up to the cabin."

"What time did you come back?"

Harley looked at his watch. "Why, I've been here in the hotel for about an hour and a half, I guess, perhaps two hours."

"She hasn't been home. I was rather expecting her."

"She said she had an appointment she'd forgotten about," Harley explained reassuringly. "She was speeding up a bit to get me here. . . . Won't you sit down, Mr. Blane?"

"I feel that I've put you to a lot of trouble," Blane apologized. "I shouldn't have disturbed you. I—"

Harley laughed. "I was just digesting some of the health I absorbed up at your cabin this afternoon. I think it's the first time I've really relaxed."

Blane nodded in mechanical acquiescence, his mind apparently occupied with something else. Then suddenly he shot a quick glance at Harley. "How'd you like to stay up there for a few days?"

"At the cabin?"

"Yes."

13

"Why—wouldn't that inconvenience you?"

"Not at all."

"I understood you had a meeting—"

"I'd prefer to hold it at my house. I'd like to have you up there, Harley. Of course, you'd have to do your own cooking, but—"

Harley smiled as Blane hesitated. "If you're really serious, there's nothing I'd like better."

"See anyone up at the cabin this afternoon?" Blane asked, trying to make his voice sound casual.

"Why, yes. Jack Hardisty came up there."

Blane gnawed at his close-clipped, gray moustache. "Notice anything strange about him?" he asked abruptly.

Harley said, "His manner seemed to be much the same as usual."

"Yes, yes, I know," Blane said. "Reminds you of a firecracker trying to pretend it's a cannon. I want you to do something for me. You'll be well paid, and a little later on, we can talk about something permanent. I want you to go up to that cabin now, tonight. Keep an eye on anything that goes on up there."

Harley hesitated.

Blane, noticing that hesitancy, said, "You can rest assured that whatever compensation—"

"It isn't that," Harley interpolated. "I'm wondering exactly what I'm supposed to do."

Blane said, "I'll tell you a secret. Adele doesn't know it. Milicent doesn't know. . . . Jack Hardisty is short ten thousand dollars over at the Roxbury bank. Adele probably told you that. Here's what she *doesn't* know. Jack expected, of course, I'd make his shortage good in case he was discovered, and hush the whole thing up. I fooled him. I told him I was damned if I was going to. . . . Damned little pipsqueak! I don't consider him one of the family. I know how it would hurt Milicent to have a scandal like that, but it's better to have it happen

14

now and get it over with. He's just a cunning little adventurer who insinuated himself into the family by sweeping Milicent off her feet. Milicent hadn't had much attention paid to her by the local boys. She'd never had any experience with what we call fortune hunters. . . . I didn't have the heart to tell her. No one did. . . . You *couldn't* tell her. There was just a chance Jack really was all wrapped up in her. He said he was. She thought he was. She wanted him—oh, well, you're not interested in all this."

Harley started to say something, but Blane held up his hand. "Here's the low-down. I told Hardisty I wasn't going to make good. He could face the music. . . . Know what he did?"

Harley shook his head.

"That's what comes of not having him thrown in jail like a common criminal. He cleaned out everything in the bank—about ninety thousand dollars in cash. Then he telephoned me and told me what he'd done; said that if I wanted to make good the ten thousand, I'd get the rest of the assets back; that if he was going to jail he'd as soon be hung for a sheep as a lamb, and he was going to make it worth his while. He'd have a stake when he came out. . . . That's the kind of a cur he is.

"If he went up to the cabin, he quite probably went up there to find a hiding place for the stuff. If he's buried it there, we'll have to find it. How about going up and—"

Harley Raymand opened the closet door, pulled out his coat.

"I'm ready to start any time, Mr. Blane."

Blane said, "You haven't had dinner. You go to the dining room and get yourself some dinner. Don't hurry. It will be at least an hour or an hour and a half before I'm ready to leave. I'll drive you up there myself. Just take your time. . . . I'd appreciate it if you'd be waiting

15

in the lobby so you can hop right in when I come back. . . . And I'm deeply grateful, my boy. Having you up there will take a load off my mind."

3

The cabin was more isolated than ever at night. The absolute silence out on the porch made one conscious of his ears, set up a vague ringing rhythm within the eardrums. The blazing stars seemed to hang just above the tops of the pine trees. Harley had the feeling that he could stand on the porch with a .22 rifle and shoot them down, as though they were lighted Christmas tree ornaments hanging from the dome of the sky.

The evening had turned chill, with that peculiar penetrating cold which comes at night in the high places, which gets into the blood and settles around the marrow of the bones.

Mr. Blane had left at once, and Harley laid a fire in the wood stove and lit it. The dry pine crackled into cheery flame. When the warmth touched him, Harley realized how cold he had really been, and began to shiver. He took blankets from the windowseat in the front room, and made up a bed on the spring cot on the front porch.

He had returned to the warmth of the fire, when a board on the porch creaked. Listening, he felt certain he heard the sound of cautious steps.

Harley slipped through the doorway into the kitchen, closing the connecting door to shut out the light, and stood with his face pressed against the window.

There was someone on the porch, someone who moved with catlike stealth, trying to peer through the side windows without being seen.

Harley tried in vain to recognize the figure. He closed his eyes for a few seconds to adjust them to the darkness. When he opened them again, the figure was still there peering in at the side window. Apparently the man had found a crack of visibility between the drapes, because Harley could see a very faint line of light across his face, a thread-like strip which looked as though it had been ruled with a luminous pencil.

When Harley was on the point of going out to challenge the intruder, he saw the figure move cautiously around to the front of the house.

"Hallooooooo! Anybody home?"

The voice was almost instantly swallowed up in the unechoing silence.

Harley went at once to stand by the front door, but didn't open it.

"Who is it?" he called.

"There's been an accident."

"Where?"

"Down the road a piece."

"Were you hurt?"

"No, but I need your help."

Harley flung open the door.

The man who stood facing him was twenty-seven or twenty-eight years old. He had a somewhat whimsical smile, but his eyes stared with disconcerting steadiness. The mouth was well formed, the hair black and tangled, pushed back and partially held in place by a broad-brimmed, battered felt hat. He was short—not over five feet three or four inches—and slender, but he carried himself with an air, and his motions indicated a hard, muscled body.

17

"I didn't know anyone was living here," he explained apologetically.

"I haven't been here very long," Harley admitted, and then added quickly, "You seem familiar with the property."

The other laughed. "I'm a next-door neighbor—in a way of speaking. My cabin's on down the road half a mile."

Harley extended his hand, introduced himself. The other said, "I'm Burton Strague. I'm a writer of sorts. My sister and I have rented the Brigham cabin. We're heating it with rejection slips."

"I think I know the place," Harley said. "Won't you come in?"

"Thanks, but I'm looking for help. A car went off the road down here. I was going up to see if Rod Beaton would come along and give us a hand. Then I saw your light and wondered who was in here. The cabin hasn't been tenanted for months. . . . Belongs to a Vincent Blane, doesn't it?"

"Yes. . . . Who's this other man you mentioned?"

"Rodney Beaton, the artist, naturalist and wild-life photographer. It was through him we came up here. I became acquainted with him by correspondence. He bought one of the cabins up here not very long ago. . . . How about coming along and giving a hand with that car?"

"How far is it," Harley asked, and then added quickly by way of explanation, "I'm convalescing."

The other looked at him quickly, sudden respect in his eyes.

"Army?"

"Yes."

"Gosh, how I wanted to go, but I'm T.B. All right, I guess, as long as I stay quiet, but—a man hates to stay quiet while there's shooting going on. . . . That accident's

18

about a quarter of a mile down the road. You hadn't better tackle it if you're not feeling fit. It's getting a little crimpy outside."

"A quarter of a mile," Harley said. "That would put it right down—"

"Just beyond where this road joins the main highway. Fellow must have been going pretty fast and missed the curve. A two-tone blue job. I don't think anyone's under it, but we ought to make sure. We'll have to get help to lift the car. That's why I'm—"

"I'll go," Harley said, trying to keep expression from his face as he realized the description of the car was that of the one Jack Hardisty had been driving. "You don't think the driver's pinned under the car?"

"I doubt it," Strague said. "Sis is staying down there so in case there are any sounds of life under the car she can tell the injured driver help is on the way. If you want to go down, I'll run up to Beaton's place and we'll join you within a half hour."

"All right," Harley said, "I'll start just as soon as I get on my coat and take a look at the fire."

Harley went back to the kitchen and closed the dampers on the stove. He returned to the front room, turned off the gasoline lantern, belted his heavy overcoat about him and took the precaution of locking up. He slipped a flashlight in his pocket and started down the roadway.

As he descended into the little draw, it became measurably colder. Occasionally he used the beam of his flashlight to guide him through some shadowed twist in the road. Then, almost before he knew it, he was at the intersection with the main road. . . . If a car had gone off, it must have been right at the turn, about ten yards below. . . . A two-tone blue job. That certainly sounded like Jack Hardisty's automobile.

Raymand switched on his flashlight, holding the beam down in the road, looking for tracks. He found, without

19

difficulty, where the car had gone off. The tracks were plain, once you started looking for them, although he certainly hadn't noticed them when Mr. Blane had driven him up to the cabin. . . . In a way, he shouldn't have left that cabin. And yet, if this should turn out to be Jack Hardisty's car, and—

"Yoohoo," a feminine voice called from the darkness down below the bank.

"Hello," Harley called. "Are you Miss Strague?"

"Yes."

He saw her, then, standing about halfway down a steep declivity, her shoulder resting against a tall pine. "You hadn't better try coming straight down," she warned. "You can go down the road about twenty or thirty yards and work your way down a little ridge. Even then you'll have to be careful."

Harley said, "Your brother and the man he went to get should show up soon. I'm from the Blane cabin up here. . . . How far is the wreck from where you're standing?"

"It's directly below me, thirty or forty feet. I don't think anyone's in it."

Harley walked down the road and found the sharp ridge the girl had mentioned. Even with the aid of his flashlight, it took him several minutes to get down to join Burton Strague's sister.

She was tall and slender. He could tell that much about her, although he couldn't see her features distinctly, much as he wanted to. Courtesy demanded he keep the beam of his flashlight from her eyes. Her voice sounded cultured, the voice of a young woman who is well poised and very certain of herself.

Harley Raymand introduced himself. He tried to avoid mentioning his military service, but he felt the searching gaze of her eyes. Then she said suddenly, "Oh yes, you're from the Army. I should have known. You're the man we read about in the Kenvale paper."

Harley tried to detour the subject by moving over to where he could inspect the car. It was Jack Hardisty's car beyond question. It was lying on its top, the wheels in the air, the body jammed down between huge boulders.

"I haven't heard the faintest sound," Lola Strague said. "If anyone's in it, he must be dead. . . . So you're *the* Harley Raymand I've been reading about!"

There followed ten or fifteen minutes during which Harley found himself answering polite, adroit, but pointed, questions. Then they heard the sound of an automobile on the road above, the slamming of a car door. Someone stumbled, and a little rock rolled and clattered down the steep slope to plunge with a rattling escort of loose gravel to a final resting place in the canyon.

"Cease firing," Lola Strague called with a laugh. "Did you bring an ax?"

Burt Strague's voice sounded from above. "I brought an ax, a flashlight, and a rope from the house. I couldn't get Rod. There's a note on his door saying he's gone to town for the evening. I waited five or ten minutes, hanging around the place, hoping he'd show up. . . . Did Mr. Raymand find you?"

"I'm here," Harley Raymand called.

"Well, I think the three of us can do the job. I'll double the rope around a tree and slide down it. Look out, here I come. I—wait a minute, I think I hear a car coming."

They listened, and could hear the sound of an automobile coming rapidly up the grade. Then, after a moment, they saw the reflections of headlights shining against the tops of trees, shifting from the bank on the left of the grade to the dark abyss of blackness which marked the canyon. A few moments later the headlights steadied, to send a stream of brilliant illumination flowing directly along the road above. The motor abruptly changed its tempo. There was the sound of brakes and then Burt Strague's voice calling, "I wonder if you can give us a hand. There's a car down here and—"

Masculine laughter boomed from above. There was the sound of a car door slamming, then a deep bass voice said, "Well, don't be so damned formal about it."

Lola Strague said, parenthetically, to Harley Raymand, "That's Rod Beaton now. He must be coming back from town."

A woman's voice said, "Why, hello, Burt."

"Hello, Myrna."

Lola Strague added, "Myrna Payson," and with sudden bitterness, "our local glamour girl."

From the road above there drifted down low-voiced conversation, the boom of Rodney Beaton's heavy laughter. Harley Raymand caught also the tinkle of Myrna Payson's light laugh. Standing in the darkness, apparently forgotten by those above, Harley had an opportunity to appreciate the significance of what Lola Strague had said. Myrna Payson's presence seemed to distract the attention of both men from the car at the bottom of the canyon and the people who waited there.

Lola Strague made no further comment, but in the rigid formality of her seething silence, Harley Raymand could feel her anger.

For what seemed almost two minutes, the little group up on the roadway chatted and laughed. Then Harley Raymand saw a broad-shouldered giant silhouetted against the illumination of the headlights. Rodney Beaton, standing on the edge of the embankment, looking down into the darkness called good-naturedly, "What have you got down there?"

"A wrecked car," Lola Strague said crisply, and added nothing whatever to those three essential words.

At the tone of her voice, Rodney Beaton seemed suddenly anxious to make amends for his apparent neglect. He became instantly the energetic executive, assuming complete control.

"All right, Burt, you say you have a rope. Let's double it around this tree. I'll slide down it and you can follow. Then we'll pull the rope down after us. . . . You'd better stay here and watch the road, Myrna."

Beaton's voice was quietly authoritative. He somehow had the knack of getting things done. The scene almost instantly became efficiently active.

Rodney Beaton came down the rope first, sliding and slipping directly down the steep declivity, sending a shower of loose gravel rattling on ahead of him. Burt Strague followed, and Myrna Payson came to the edge of the roadway to stand outlined against the illumination reflected back from the car's headlights.

Harley Raymand had a confused overlapping of impressions: the young woman standing up on the side of the roadway; the headlights faintly silhouetting her figure through her clothes, an attractive young woman who might not have been entirely unaware that the illumination was turning her skirt into a shadow gown—Burt Strague, slender, seeming somehow inefficient as he floundered and scrambled down the rope, his feet shooting out from under him on two or three occasions—Rodney Beaton, a good-natured giant, making every move count. . . . Then Lola Strague was performing introductions and Harley's hand was gripped by Rodney Beaton's powerful fingers.

Harley saw that Beaton was some ten years older than Burt Strague. He was tall, powerful, loose-jointed, not fat, but thick. He had a smiling mouth, a firm jaw, and was wearing a western hat of the type generally referred to as a "five gallon."

In the light reflected from the beam of the five-cell flashlight Rod Beaton was holding, Harley had a chance to get a better look at Lola Strague. She was blonde, not more than twenty-two or twenty-three, attired in a heavy checkered woolen shirt, open low at the throat, a plaid woolen jacket, trousers and laced boots. She gave the impression of being quite competently a part of the outdoors, of wearing clothes that were warm, strong, and made for service.

The beam of the flashlight darted down into the black canyon, licked over boulders and fallen trees, then came to rest on the overturned car.

Rod Beaton seemed thoroughly at home, thoroughly capable of handling a situation such as that. He said, "We won't try any salvage work, just make sure there's no one in the car and then quit. . . . I think we can cut down the tree, Burt. If you'll hold the flashlight, I'll swing the ax. We'll use it as a lever and raise the car so we can see the interior."

Strague held the flashlight. Beaton swung the light ax with a smooth rhythm of powerful shoulders, the gleaming blade biting deep into the wood with every swing. It seemed to Harley that it took no more than four or five swinging blows to sever the tree neatly through. Then Beaton trimmed off the little limbs and the top, and had a pole some fifteen feet long and ten inches in diameter at the butt.

Calmly, competently, he assumed command, issuing quiet instructions, treating Harley Raymand with the same assurance he displayed toward Burt and Lola Strague.

"Now, Raymand, if you'll get out on the far end of that pole. Just sit on it. Don't try to use that bad elbow. . . . Burt, you and Lola get on each side as near the end as you can. Let me guide this end of it. . . . All right, now put a little pressure on it."

They came down on the end of the pole. The car groaned and scraped, then raised up. Beaton blocked it with rocks, said, "All right. Take the pressure off the

24

pole. Let me give you a new purchase. . . . Okay, here we go again."

Once more the car moved.

Beaton said, "We can see in it now," and the beam of his spotlight showed windows that were cobwebbed with glass fractures and illuminated an empty interior.

"No one in here," Beaton said. "Let's take a look and see if he was thrown clear."

The flashlight swung around in ever widening circles.

"No sign of him," Beaton said.

Abruptly Harley asked, "Can you get a good look at the interior of that car, Beaton, and see if there's a spade in there?"

At the sudden, complete silence which greeted his request, Harley realized how peculiar it sounded.

"You see," he added, by way of explanation, "I think I know that car. If it's the one I think it is, there should be a spade in back of the front seat."

"Okay, I'll take a look," Beaton said. "You don't know the license number?"

"No," Raymand added somewhat lamely. "It was a car that was up at the cabin this afternoon."

"I see. . . . No, there doesn't seem to be any spade in it."

Lola Strague said, "Well, we've discharged our duties as Good Samartians. I guess there's nothing to do now except get back to the road."

Rodney Beaton climbed up the steep slope as far as he could, then, coiling the rope, said to Myrna Payson, "Catch an end of this and loop it around that tree, will you, Myrna?"

With a heave of his powerful shoulders, Beaton sent the rope snaking up against the glow of the headlights, and as Myrna Payson caught the end and doubled it around the tree, she moved with a certain lithe grace, a deft co-ordination of arms and legs that accomplished her task and sent the loose end of the rope back down to Rodney Beaton in a surprisingly short time.

With the aid of the rope, they went up the steep incline to the road with relative ease.

Harley Raymand was left until last. He called up, "I'm afraid to trust this arm. I think I'd better—"

"Not at all," Beaton interrupted heartily. "Just loop the rope around your waist and knot it with a bowline. . . . Can you tie a bowline?"

"I think so," Harley said.

"Wait a minute. I'll tie one and toss it down to you."

Beaton's hands made two or three swift passes over the rope, then a loop came down to Raymand. He stepped inside it, raised it to his waist, took hold with his right hand, and leaning against the rope and using his legs, was pulled up the steep pitch.

At the top he was presented to Myrna Payson, who was, as Rodney Beaton gravely explained, a neighboring cattle rancher. One look at Myrna Payson's wide-spaced, laughing eyes, her full, vivid-red lips, and Harley knew why Rodney Beaton and Burt Strague had been so preoccupied up there on the road. Her skin showed the result of care. Her clothes followed the lines of her figure with a well-fitting grace that to a woman would mean she "could wear anything." Men would see only the effect. As Harley studied her, Myrna Payson's eyes in turn took him in from head to toe and made a careful and frankly personal appraisal of him.

In the quick burst of general conversation which followed the introduction, Harley gathered that the car, an old model coupe, belonged to Rodney Beaton; that, in the interest of "conserving rubber and gas," he had "picked up his neighbor" in the early evening for a trip to town. Harley also gathered that Lola Strague definitely resented this. . . . Then of a sudden, Harley felt

26

too utterly wearied to remain interested in the affairs of this little group.

"I'm going to say good night, if you don't mind," he said. "I've had rather a trying day."

"Oh, but let me drive you up to your cabin," Burt Strague said quickly.

Harley didn't look forward to the walk with any degree of pleasure, yet he said, "Oh that's all right. I'd just as soon walk."

"Nonsense," Lola said firmly. "Burt will drive you up. Come on. Get in."

Lola Strague jumped into the car in the middle of the front seat. Harley climbed in beside her, and Burt twisted himself in behind the steering wheel. Rodney Beaton seemed, for a moment, ill at ease. It was as though he had hoped to get Lola Strague off to one side for a word in private before leaving. But Myrna Payson called out, "Come on, Rod. We've got to get our car out of the way so they can turn around."

Beaton still hesitated.

Burt Strague said, "The nearest telephone is at the ranger station three miles up that road, Rod. I'll drive Raymand up to his cabin. You might go on up to the ranger station and notify the sheriff."

After that it seemed a good five seconds before Beaton said, "I guess that's the thing to do. Good night, everyone."

No one tried to make conversation as Burt Strague piloted the car up to the cabin. And Harley was glad of it. He felt too tired even to talk.

They deposited him in front of the cabin. Burt said good night, and added something about hoping to see more of him and trusting the experience hadn't been too much for him. Lola Strague gave him her hand, said, "Hope you'll be all right, and we'll be seeing you again."

There was someting of finality in her comments, but

Burt waited for two or three seconds, then said, "Well, good night," and turned the car.

Harley felt positive that Burt had been hoping for an invitation to come in.

Harley, climbing the three steps to the porch, realized that once more he was completely exhausted. He had intended to look for the buried clock, but felt able to do no more than crawl into the bed he had made out on the porch. He fell asleep almost instantly.

It was an hour before sunrise when he opened his eyes to find the air crisp with cold. He snuggled down into the warm blankets and amused himself by fastening his eyes upon one particular star, trying to keep it from receding to nothing in the growing light. But the star eluded him, vanished, and Harley couldn't find it again. Smiling drowsily over his failure, he drifted off to sleep once more. The sun was warm on the porch when he finally awakened.

Harley knew as soon as he threw back the covers that he was feeling much stronger. The fresh mountain air had drained poisons from his system, and for the first time in weeks he actually wanted food—and lots of it.

He lit the oil stove, cooked coffee, eggs, bacon, toast and cereal—and then thought of the buried clock.

While the dishwater was heating, Harley went out to the porch, and then walked down the sloping, needle-carpeted grounds. He found the spot he wanted without difficulty and swept away the covering of pine needles.

The clock was ticking merrily away.

Harley compared it with his watch.

The clock was still exactly twenty-five minutes slow.

Harley replaced the box, carefully put the pine needles and moss back into place and returned to the cabin. The water was not yet hot enough for the dishes. There were no dishtowels in sight, but Harley remembered that linen was stored in a big cedar chest in the back bedroom. He opened the door of the bedroom, conscious of the fact that the chill of the night still clung to this room on the north side of the house. He was half-way to the cedar chest before he noticed that the bed was occupied.

For what must have been several seconds, Harley stood motionless with surprise, not knowing whether to withdraw quietly or to speak. Suppose Milicent or Adele had gone to the cabin, exhausted, had climbed into bed, knowing nothing of his subsequent arrival. Harley could sense complications.

The sleeper was facing the window, away from the door. The covers were pulled up in such a way that the head was completely concealed. Harley decided to get it over with.

"Good morning!"

The figure didn't move.

Harley raised his voice, "I don't want to intrude, but I'd like to know who you are." The figure gave no sign of having heard.

Harley walked over to the bed, let his hand fall on the covers over the shoulder—and instantly knew something was radically wrong. . . . He jerked with his right arm, pulling the motionless form toward him.

It was Jack Hardisty.

He had been dead for hours.

4

Perry Mason hummed a little tune as he strolled down the corridor to his office, moving with the leisurely, long-legged rhythm characteristic of him. Walking to meet the adventures of the day, he didn't intend to be too hurried to enjoy them.

He latchkeyed the door of his private office, and caught Della Street's smile as she looked up from the mail.

"What ho!" Mason said. "Another day. . . . How about the dollar, Chancellor of the Exchequer."

Della Street bowed with mock humility. "The dollar awaits, my lord."

Mason lost his bantering tone. "Don't tell me you've scared up a new case."

"We have a potential client."

"In the outer office?"

"No. He's not the type who waits in outer offices." Della Street consulted a memorandum on her desk. "He's a Mr. Vincent P. Blane, a banker and department store owner at Kenvale. He called on long distance, three times within thirty minutes. The first two times he wouldn't talk with anyone except Perry Mason. The third time he consented to talk with Mr. Mason's secretary."

Mason hung his hat in the closet, crossed over to the big desk, selected a cigarette from the office humidor, and said, "I don't like him."

"Why not?"

"He sounds pot-bellied and self-important. What does he want?"

"His son-in-law was murdered in a mountain cabin sometime last night."

Mason scraped a match on the under side of the desk, devoted his attention to lighting the cigarette before asking, "Who's elected as the official suspect?"

"No one."

"Who's nominated?"

"They haven't even made a nomination."

"Then what the devil does Blane want *me* for? I'm not a detective, I'm a lawyer."

She smiled. "It seems there are several family skeletons Mr. Blane wants kept safely in the closet. Naturally, he didn't dare say much on the phone. Both of Mr. Blane's daughters were up at the cabin yesterday afternoon. Mr. Blane himself was also up there. . . . And well, after all, the man has money."

Mason said, "Oh, I suppose I've got to handle it, but it sounds like a legal chore, one of these uninspiring, routine family murders."

Della Street once more consulted her memorandum. "There is, however, one redeeming feature," she added, her eyes twinkling.

"Della, you've been holding out on me!" Mason charged.

"No. I only saved the dessert until last."

"All right, let's have the dessert."

"A buried clock," she said, "which is running about twenty-five minutes slow. It's buried somewhere near the cabin where the murder was committed, a small-edition alarm clock in a lacquered box. It—"

Mason started for the cloak closet.

He called to Della Street as he grabbed his hat. "The clock does it. . . . Come on. Let's go!"

31

5

Mason was advised in Kenvale that the deputy sheriff, a representative of the coroner, Vincent Blane and Harley Raymand had left for the scene of the crime only a few minutes earlier; that Mason could probably catch up with them if he "stepped on it."

Mason duly stepped on it, arriving at the cabin just as the little group was getting ready to leave the chill north bedroom where the body lay just as Raymand had left it.

Mason was acquainted with Jameson, the deputy sheriff, and so was permitted to join the group without question, a tribute to Mason's reputation as well as Blane's local influence.

The lawyer had a glimpse of a cold bedroom, rustic furniture, knotty pine walls, clothes thrown over a chair, shoes placed at the side of the bed, and the stiff, still form of the little man, who, in his lifetime, had tried so desperately to be a magnetic, dominant personality. Now, in death, he seemed shriveled to his true stature, a cold corpse in a cold bedroom.

Mason made a swift survey of the room. "Don't touch anything," the deputy warned.

"I won't," Mason assured him, studying the room carefully.

"He must have undressed, gone to sleep and been killed while he was sleeping," the coroner's representative said.

The deputy sheriff said, "Well he's dead, all right, and

32

it's murder. I'm going to close this room up and leave things just as they are until someone from the Los Angeles office can get here. . . . Now, let's take a look at this buried clock—although I don't see where it enters into the picture."

The deputy ushered them out of the room, closed and locked the door, and followed Harley out to the warmth of the sloping, sun-bathed clearing.

Harley walked over to the granite rocks. "Now, the clock is buried right about here. You can hear it ticking if you listen."

"Let's take a look," the deputy sheriff said.

Harley got down on his knees, scraped away moss and pine needles. He placed his ear to the ground, then straightened and looked puzzled. "I'm certain this is the place," he said.

The deputy's tone was frankly skeptical. "Doesn't look as though anything had ever been buried there."

"Perhaps it's a little deeper," Blane suggested.

Harley, scraping a wider clearing in the ground, said, "No, the lid of the box was quite close to the surface."

The deputy sheriff kicked the ground with the toe of his boot. "Doesn't look to me as if this place had been disturbed since last winter."

Harley bent over once more to place his ear against the ground.

The deputy sheriff flashed a glance at the coroner's representative.

"I don't hear it ticking now," Harley said.

"You're certain about that clock?"

Harley flushed. "I had it in my hands, took it out of the box. Adele Blane can vouch for that."

Jameson seemed reluctant to extend belief. "And it was there this morning?" he asked.

"Yes."

"*After* you'd found the body?"

33

"No, just before I found the body."

"But after Hardisty had been killed?"

"Oh yes."

"Well," the deputy said, in the tone of one who wishes to be rid of a matter which may prove embarrassing, "then Jack Hardisty couldn't have taken it, and that's pretty apt to mean it isn't connected with the murder. Now, how about Hardisty's car. You haven't any idea how it got down in that canyon?"

"No."

"Now, I'm just asking this as a question," Jameson said. "There's no call to get up on your ear about it, but it's a question I want you to answer, and answer truthfully. You won't have a second chance at this, Raymand. Your answer's got to stand for all time. . . . You didn't get on the running board of Jack Hardisty's automobile, get it going at a good clip, then step off the running board and let the car go over the grade, did you?"

"Absolutely not."

"Why did Blane ask you to stay up here at the cabin?"

"He wanted the place watched."

"Why was that, Mr. Blane?" the deputy asked.

Before Blane could answer, Harley Raymand said, with a smile, "I think it was an attempt on Mr. Blane's part to be magnanimous. He thought a period of rest and recuperation up here at the cabin would do me good, and he tried to make a job out of it so I wouldn't feel under obligations to him."

Blane started to say something, then apparently changing his mind, smiled enigmatically. After a moment he said, "Now if you'll excuse me, while you're getting additional details from Harley, I'll have a chat with Mr. Mason."

Blane motioned to Mason, and the lawyer, Della Street and Blane walked around the big granite outcropping to a sequestered clearing where they were out of earshot.

34

"Mr. Mason," Blane said, "I can't begin to tell you how relieved I am now that you're here. Thank you for coming."

"The buried clock did it," Mason told him. "What do *you* know about that clock?"

"Harley Raymand mentioned it to me for the first time this morning. Adele confirmed his story. The clock was there, all right."

"There where he had scraped away the pine needles?" Mason asked.

"Raymand *may* have mistaken the place," Blane admitted.

"All right, that can wait. Tell me just what you want me to do and why you want me to do it. Hit the high spots. That deputy will be back here in a minute with more questions."

Blane spoke with nervous rapidity, all but running his words together, in his anxiety to give Mason the picture.

"Jack Hardisty was my son-in-law—married Millicent. She was a girl who wanted a career—studied nursing. She's clever—the sort people always praise for their intellect. . . . Then along came Jack Hardisty, handed her a new line—the passionate, fervid, romantic line—swept her off her feet, married her. Put him in a bank over at Roxbury—a damned four-flusher, a half-pint of nothing. Been breaking Milicent's heart, chasing around with a milliner over there—ten thousand short in his accounts —found it out and told him to face the music. . . . Before I could do anything about it, he took a couple of suitcases and cleaned out everything in the bank, nearly ninety thousand altogether. Rang me up, told me if I made good the ten thousand I'd get the rest of it back. If I didn't, there wouldn't be a dime in the bank when it opened this morning."

"What did you do?" Mason asked.

35

"What *could* I do?" Blaine asked. "I was stuck for it."

"How about the bonding company?"

"That's just it. The bonding company held off on his bond. There'd been a little something in Jack's past. At the time I thought the bonding company was being too damn technical—told them to go ahead and write the bond, and I'd guarantee they never lost a penny on it—signed a paper to that effect. . . . Damn fool—serves me right."

"All right. Go ahead."

"My other daughter, Adele, came up here with Harley Raymand yesterday afternoon. Before they left, Jack Hardisty showed up. He didn't see them. Raymand says Hardisty had a spade in the car. . . . They started back for Kenvale and met Milicent on the road. She asked if Jack was up here.

"Adele didn't think much of that until after Milicent had started on for the cabin. Then she got frightened. She told Harley she had another appointment, rushed him to his hotel, turned around and dashed up here to the cabin."

"After Milicent?" Mason asked.

Blane nodded.

"Find her?"

"Yes."

"Here at the cabin?"

"No, down by the main highway."

"What was she doing there?"

"Having a spell of nerves."

"Where was her husband?"

"No one knows. Milicent hadn't gone to the cabin. She'd parked her car at a wide place in the road, and started to walk up to the cabin."

"Why not drive all the way up?"

"She told Adele she didn't want her husband to hear her coming."

"Did she say why?"

"No."

"All right, she didn't get to the cabin?"

"No, her nerves went back on her. She must have had hysterics. She had a gun in her purse. She dropped it over the embankment at the edge of the road."

"Why?"

"She told Adele she was afraid to trust herself with it."

"Afraid she'd use it on herself, or on someone else?"

"I don't think she said."

"And Adele didn't ask?"

"I don't know. I don't think so."

"Revolver or automatic?"

"Revolver."

"Hers?"

"Yes. It's one I gave her. She was nervous and had to stay alone a lot at night. Her husband was away a lot of the time."

"All right. She threw the gun away. Then what?"

"Adele got her to promise to go on back to Kenvale and stay with her."

"Did she do it?"

"No."

"Why not. What happened?"

"We don't know. Adele drove on in her car. Milicent was right behind until they got to Kenvale. Then in the traffic, Adele lost her. It was getting dark and the headlights had been turned on. That makes it hard to watch a car behind, after you get in traffic."

"Adele lost her—so what? Did Milicent go to your house?"

"No. So far as I can learn, no one has seen her. Adele was watching the car in the rear-view mirror—other headlights cut in, and—well that's all."

"To whom has Adele told this?" Mason asked.

"I am the only one, so far. We want to know—"

37

Mason interrupted. "The deputy's getting ready to come back over this way. Does anyone know Milicent is missing?"

"No."

"When will they find out?"

"It may be some time. . . . I told Adele to tell the housekeeper Milicent was hysterical last night, that Adele gave her a sleeping tablet and put her to bed in the back bedroom upstairs—that Milicent isn't to be disturbed by anyone. That will stall things along until we can find her."

Mason said, "I'm not certain that what you've done is for Milicent's best interest."

"Why not? If they find out we don't know where she is—"

"I understand, but amateurs shouldn't try doctoring evidence. We haven't time to discuss it now. They're coming over this way. Get the deputy sheriff off to one side and tell him about that shortage."

Blane's face showed surprise. "Why, that's one of the things I wanted you to do—to keep that hushed up, to tell me how I—"

"You can't keep that hushed up," Mason interrupted. "Try to cover that up and let them catch you at it, and they'll blow the lid off."

"But I don't want—"

"Right now," Mason said, "I'm thinking of Milicent and you *should* be. Get the deputy sheriff off to one side, tell him you're giving him the information in strict confidence; that you don't want him to tell a soul."

"Well—all right—if you say so."

"Where's Adele?"

"At home."

"She know you sent for me?"

"Yes."

"Where's the nearest telephone?"

38

"Up the road about three miles there's a little settlement, a ranger station and—"

"Okay, go talk with the deputy. Here he comes now; then meet me at the Kenvale Hotel *as soon as you can get away from here.* Try to follow me within fifteen or twenty minutes."

The deputy sheriff was walking toward them. His manner was that of a man who has made up his mind to do something and wants to get it over with.

Mason said in a low voice, out of the corner of his mouth, as though coaching an actor, "Beat him to the punch. Beat him to the punch, Blane."

Blane raised his voice. "Oh, Jameson, I want to talk with you for a few minutes—privately, please."

The deputy glanced at the others, said, "Well, all right."

Mason turned to Della Street. "Come on, Della. This way." He led her around toward the back of the house, then along a well-defined trail running down a dry wash, deep enough so that they were invisible from the cabin. After they had gone a hundred yards, they scrambled up out of the wash, swung around to the place where Mason had parked his car.

Mason said, "I don't want them to hear the sound of the motor, Della. Put it in high, turn on the ignition, push the clutch pedal down. I'll start pushing it toward that grade. Let the clutch in when I tell you—after the car gets to going at a pretty good rate of speed. . . . Okay now, swing that wheel."

Mason pushed the car until it began to coast down the grade, then jumped in beside Della Street. When the car was running along at a good rate, he said, "All right, ease in the clutch."

The engine purred into smooth power.

"Make time up to that settlement," Mason said. "I want to telephone."

"I take it we're not conserving rubber?" Della asked.

"We're conserving a reputation," Mason told her.

They made the three miles of mountain road to the telephone in just a little over three and a half minutes. Mason found a telephone booth in the store, called Vincent Blane's residence in Kenvale, asked for Adele.

A few moments later, he heard a feminine voice on the line saying dubiously, "Yes, what is it, please?"

"This is Perry Mason. Know anything about me?"

"Why . . . yes."

"All right. No need to mention details. You knew your father was going to send for me."

"Yes."

"Know why?"

"Yes."

Mason said, "Your father told me about the upstairs bedroom—you understand?"

"The person who's supposed to be in it?"

"That's right."

"I understand."

Mason said, "I don't like it."

"Why not?" she asked.

"It's dangerous. We don't know what trumps are— yet. I want you to do something."

"What?"

"Go where you won't be questioned. Get out, and get out fast. Simply disappear."

"For how long?"

"Until I tell you to come back."

"How will you reach me?"

Mason said, "My secretary, Miss Della Street, will be registered at the Kenvale Hotel. Call her about five o'clock tonight. Don't mention any names over the phone. She won't mention names. If the coast is clear, she'll manage to let you know. If she doesn't let you know, it means the coast isn't clear. After five, keep calling her every few hours. . . . Got that straight?"

"Yes, Mr. Mason."

"All right, get started—and don't tell a soul where you're going. Fix things so you can't be traced. . . . And be certain to call Miss Della Street."

"I have it all straight," she said. "Good-by."

Mason hung up the receiver, waited a moment, then called his office in Los Angeles.

When the girl at Mason's switchboard answered, central said, "Deposit fifty-five cents for three minutes, please, including the Federal tax."

Mason fumbled in his pockets, opened the door of the telephone booth, called to the man behind the counter. "I've got a Los Angeles call in. My party's on the line. I need fifty-five cents. Can you give me some change?"

Mason waved a dollar bill. The man rang up NO SALE in the cash register, pulled out three twenty-five cent pieces, two dimes and a nickel, and came trotting over to the booth.

Mason thanked him, closed the door of the booth, dropped in the coins and heard the voice of Gertie, the tall, good-natured girl at the switchboard, saying, with her customary breezy informality, "Good Heavens, Mr. Mason, why didn't you just tell them to reverse the charge? Then you wouldn't have had to bother about the coins."

Mason chuckled. "Because, in the course of an investigation that may be made, the officers will wonder why I went tearing up here to put in a telephone call. Then they'll talk with the storekeeper and know my call was to my office in Los Angeles."

Gertie hestiated a moment, then said, "I get it, your *second* call."

"That's right. Only it won't occur to *them* there were two. Be a good girl, Gertie."

"Thank you, Mr. Mason. Shall we indulge in the usual

41

comments about the percentage there is in it, or have we talked long enough?"

Mason said, "We've talked long enough. You know all the answers anyway," and hung up.

6

At the hotel in Kenvale, Mason gave Della Street swift instructions. "Just before we turned off the main road, I noticed a road sign put up by the Auto Club bearing the words, '*Kern County.*' Look up the exact location of the county line and of that cabin. Then come back here and hold the fort."

"On my way," she said. "It shouldn't take long."

Mason made himself comfortable in the lobby of the hotel, watching the door, waiting for Vincent Blane. At the end of thirty impatient minutes, he went to a telephone booth and put through a person-to-person call for Paul Drake, head of the Drake Detective Agency in Los Angeles. The call was completed within a few seconds, and when Mason heard Drake's voice on the line, he said, "Perry Mason, Paul. I'm suspicious of telephones so you'll have to dot the *i's* and cross the *t's*."

"Okay, go ahead."

"I'm in Kenvale. About twenty miles from here, in the mountains, a man by the name of Blane has a cabin. Blane's son-in-law, Jack Hardisty, got himself bumped off in that cabin sometime last night. Jameson, the resident deputy sheriff who's on the job now, is inclined to be decent. There are replacements coming from Los Angeles

42

who will be hard boiled. I'd like to get everything lined up before they clam up."

"What do you mean by everything?"

"Time of death, clues, means of death, motives, opportunities, alibis—and locate Milicent Hardisty, the widow of the victim."

Drake said, "Is that last job a bit of routine?"

"No."

"You mean it may be difficult?"

"Yes."

"That's the *i* I'm supposed to dot?"

"Also the *t* you're to cross. There's a probability it may have to be a double cross."

"I take it there's no use looking in the usual places?"

"Right—and don't be fooled by information to the contrary."

"Okay Perry, where will you be?"

"Kenvale Hotel, at least until we get things straightened out. If I'm not here, Della will be."

"Who's your client?"

"Vincent P. Blane."

"Any chance that he did it?"

"The police haven't said so."

Drake said, "That doesn't answer my question."

"You just think it doesn't."

Mason hung up the telephone, waited another five minutes, then impatiently called the Blane residence.

"This is Perry Mason, the lawyer," he said to the feminine voice who answered the telephone. "Is Miss Adele Blane there?"

"No, sir."

"You're the housekeeper?"

"Yes, sir. Martha Stevens."

Mason said, "Mr. Blane was to meet me here in the hotel. He's evidently been detained. Have you heard anything from him?"

"No, sir."

"Is Mrs. Hardisty there?"

"Yes, sir. She's here in the house, but there are strict orders that she isn't to be disturbed. She was hysterical last night, and had some sleeping tablets."

Mason smiled, said, "That's fine. I won't bother her. . . . Have there been any other calls asking for her?"

"Yes, sir."

"How many?"

"Oh, there must have been half a dozen."

"Friends?"

"No, sir. Strange voices who wouldn't leave names."

"Men or women?"

"Both."

Mason said, "All right, if you hear anything from Mr. Blane, directly or indirectly, call me at the Kenvale Hotel."

He hung up and was just leaving the telephone booth when the lobby door was pushed open explosively. A small group erupted into the lobby, Blane and Jameson in the lead. Blane's face lit up with relief as he saw Mason. Jameson kept at Blane's side as the pudgy, harassed businessman crossed over to the lawyer.

Mason kept his voice casual, as he said to Blane, "You seem to pick up more people as you keep traveling."

Blane's eyes held desperate appeal. "These are witnesses," he explained quickly. "Miss Strague and her brother and Mr. Beaton. They live up around there."

Mason said, "You folks look rather hot and flustered. How about coming up to my room where it's cool and where we can have a drink?"

The deputy said, "I'm afraid there isn't time for that, Mr. Mason. Mr. Blane has adopted a very peculiar attitude."

"What is it?"

"Miss Strague has found the weapon with which the

murder was committed. Mr. Beaton was with her at the time."

Mason, sparring for time, made a little bow to Lola Strague. "Congratulations. Evidently you did some high-class detective work. . . . May I ask where it was?"

"Lying in the pine needles on the other side of that rock near which Mr. Raymand says the clock was buried."

"We don't need to go into all that now," Jameson interjected hastily. "The point is, there's evidence linking this gun with Jack Hardisty's wife."

"Is that so?" Mason asked, his voice showing only casual interest. "What's the evidence?"

Blane nodded to Beaton.

Beaton interposed hurriedly, "Of course, gentlemen, I won't swear that it was a gun she had in her hand, but I drove past her last evening. She was standing on the main road, and had something in her hand. At the time I thought it was a wrench, that her car might have broken down. I was going to ask her if she needed help, but just then she drew her arm back and tossed this gun —if it was a gun—down into the canyon. Her face was contorted with emotion. She looked at me as I drove past, without showing the slightest sign of recognition. I doubt if she even saw me, although I raised my hat."

"What time was this?" Mason asked.

"Somewhere between six-fifteen and dark. Up in the mountains we don't bother much about time. I carry a cheap watch. Sometimes I wind it, and sometimes I don't. When it's running, I usually set it by the sun, so I'm not going to stick my neck out on a statement of time that could be twisted around by a lot of lawyers on cross-examination."

Beaton's eyes twinkled amiably at Mason, the network of crows-feet springing into quick prominence. "No hard feelings, Mr. Mason."

45

"None at all," Mason grinned. "I think you'd be a hard witness to cross-examine."

Beaton said, "Mrs. Payson was in the car with me. We were going in to Kenvale together. We went to dinner and a show. She may be able to tell you what time it was, although *she* didn't see Mrs. Hardisty toss the gun down in the canyon."

"You think this was after six?" Mason asked.

"I know it was after six-fifteen because Mrs. Payson was listening to a radio program that came on at six and went off the air at six-fifteen. She made me wait until the thing was over before she'd leave. . . . And that's as close as I can fix it."

"All this is beside the point," the deputy said. "I want to talk with Mrs. Hardisty. Blane acts as though he believed his daughter was guilty."

"Nothing of the sort," Blane retorted angrily. "I'm simply trying to protect my daughter's health."

"Well, you rushed to the telephone and got Perry Mason down here in a hurry," the deputy charged, also getting angry. "I wasn't born yesterday. I know what *that* means."

Mason smiled affably. "Well now, gentlemen," he said, "*I* wasn't born yesterday, but I'm not certain that *I* know what it means."

"It means Blane is trying to—"

"Yes?" Mason invited as the deputy stopped abruptly.

"I'm not sticking my neck out," Jameson said somewhat sullenly. "I'm just a resident deputy down here. There'll be someone on hand from the main office. . . . I've looked for them to be here before this. I—Here they come now."

The door was pushed open. Two men came barging over toward the group, moving with grim purpose like warships plowing through sea toward a convoy.

Mason said to the deputy, "Doubtless, you'll want to

46

explain the situation to these gentlemen. While you're doing that, I'll confer with my client."

He scooped his hand through Blane's arm, drew him off slightly to one side, said, "Okay, Blane, this is the pay-off."

When Blane spoke, he was so nervous his lips quivered. "It's her gun, Mason," he said. "I recognized it."

"What have you told them?"

"I've told them I would have to consult you before letting them know where my daughter was. . . . This is terrible, Mason. They'll find out that Milicent has disappeared now. There's no way we can stall it off any longer."

"You haven't any idea where she is?"

"No."

"Well, you've got to let them go to your house—and *then* bluff it out. Remember I'll be with you. When they find the darkened bedroom with a bed that hasn't been slept in, they'll start acting rough. When the going gets too tough for you, let me step in and handle it."

"All right—just so they don't jump on Adele."

"They won't."

"What makes you so certain of that?"

Mason smiled, "What did you think you'd retained counsel for? Go ahead, Blane, get it over with. . . . Here they come now."

The men from the Los Angeles office were hard boiled. They offered Blane none of the polite courtesies which the resident deputy had extended. "We want Mrs. Hardisty," the man who acted as spokesman said. "What's the idea that we can't see her?"

"I think there's been a misunderstanding," Mason interposed. "Mr. Blane knows that his daughter has been very much upset over another matter which has nothing to do with—"

"Well, we think it has a lot to do with it."

Jameson said hastily, "I've explained to these men what Mr. Blane told me. We'll try to keep it out of the papers."

"As I was endeavoring to explain," Mason went on suavely, "because of this unusual situation, Mr. Blane—"

"What's that got to do with where Mrs. Hardisty is now? Do you *know* where she is, Blane?"

Blane hesitated.

Mason said, "Go ahead, Blane. Tell them."

"She's at my house, asleep."

The spokesman turned to Jameson. "You know where his place is?"

"Yes."

"Okay, let's go."

"Got your car here?" Mason asked Blane, as the others turned away.

"Yes."

"All right, let's get there first."

Blane led the way to where his car was parked.

Mason settled down in the cushions, said nothing until Blane had parked the car in front of the house, then he said, as the officers drove up, "Remember to show surprise when they find no one in that bedroom."

They escorted the officers into the house. Blane said, "I'll go up and notify my daughter that—"

"No dice," the man from the Los Angeles office interposed. "This is a business, not a social call. We want to talk with Mrs. Hardisty before anyone talks with her, before *anyone* gives her a tip on what's happened. So suppose you just—"

"I insist," Blane said with simple dignity, "that I'm going to be there when you interview my daughter."

The Los Angeles deputy hesitated.

Mason said, "And, as attorney for Mrs. Hardisty, I am going to be on hand."

"Okay, I'm not going to have an argument about that.

I'm not going to bite her. . . . But one thing's definite: *I'm* going to do *all* the talking. If she answers my questions satisfactorily, all right. If she gets any coaching from you people, I'm going to take that into consideration in making my recommendations to the D.A. Now, show us the way to the bedroom."

Mason nodded to Blane, and Blane led the little group up the stairs and down a corridor to a closed door.

"This it?" the deputy asked.

Blane said. "Yes, this is the back bedroom."

The deputy reached toward the doorknob.

"Just a minute," Blane said. "My daughter is entitled to *some* courtesies."

Blane knocked on the door.

There was no sound from within the room.

The officer knocked, his knuckles beating a loud summons on the panels of the wood.

Mason was reaching for his cigarette case when he heard a key turn on the inside of the door, and a woman, who quite evidently had been in the process of dressing and had hurriedly thrown on a bathrobe, said, "What is it, please?"

"You're Mrs. Jack Hardisty?" the deputy asked.

"Yes. What is it, Father?"

The Los Angeles deputy said to Blane, "Okay, I'll handle it from here on."

Mrs. Hardisty showed her consternation. "Why, what's the matter?"

"Where's your husband, Mrs. Hardisty?"

"I . . . Why, I . . . Isn't he at Roxbury at the bank?"

"You know he isn't."

She was silent.

"Did you know he was short at the bank?"

Blane started to interrupt, but the officer pushed him into the background. "How about it, Mrs. Hardisty? Did you or didn't you?"

49

She glanced toward her father.

"Let's have a straight answer to the question, please. Never mind trying to get signals from anybody."

"I . . . Yes."

"That's better. When did you see him last?"

"Yesterday."

"What time yesterday?"

"I guess it was about one o'clock or one-thirty."

"Let's see if we can't do better than that, Mrs. Hardisty. You're familiar with the mountain cabin your father owns?"

"Why, yes, of course."

"You were up there yesterday afternoon, weren't you?"

"Yes."

"Why did you go up there?"

"I . . . I thought Jack might be up there."

"You went up there, then, to see your husband, didn't you?"

"Yes."

"And what time was that?"

"I don't know exactly."

"And you did see him, didn't you?"

"No."

For a moment there was a break in the rapid-fire tempo of the questions as the officer digested his surprise; then he returned to the attack, this time a little more savage, a little more grim. "Mrs. Hardisty, I'm going to be frank with you. Your answers may be very important—important to you. Now I want a *truthful* answer. You saw your husband up there at the cabin, didn't you?"

"No, I didn't. I didn't even go all the way up to the cabin. I . . . I had hysterics. I stayed down on the highway . . . Well, I walked up our road a ways. I don't know how far. I just went all to pieces—and then I came back to the main road and tried to quiet my nerves by walking, and I met Adele—"

"Who's Adele?"

"My sister."

"Why did you go to pieces? What was it you intended to do when you saw your husband?"

Mason interposed suavely, "I think that's far enough along that line, officer."

"*You* do?"

"Yes."

"As it happens, you don't have anything to say about it. I told you *I* was going to do the talking."

Mason said, "So far as questions of fact are concerned, that's quite all right. I have no objection to letting my client answer—"

"But who *is* this man?" Milicent asked in confusion. "What's this talk about me being his client?"

Mason said to the officer, "I'm going to give you every advantage. I'm not going to answer that question. I'm going to let you break the news to her in your own way, but I'm—"

"I'm doing this," the officer said angrily. "I don't *have* to do it here. I can load her in a car right now and take her in to the D.A.'s office. I've got enough on her."

"You haven't got enough on her to move her out of that room," Mason said.

"Don't you think I haven't. That gun—"

"What about the gun?" Mason asked.

The officer angrily turned back to Mrs. Hardisty, said, "Since the subject has come up, I'll ask you the question direct. Why did you take a gun up there with you?"

She was quite apparently stalling to cover her confusion. "I . . . take a gun . . . You mean—"

"I mean that you took a thirty-eight caliber revolver which your father had given you for a Christmas present up to the cabin with you when you went up to see your husband. Now *why* did you do it?"

51

Mason interposed meaningly, "The gun your father gave you for your *protection,* Mrs. Hardisty."

"I took it up because—because I was afraid of Jack."

The deputy said angrily to Mason, "Oh, no! *You* aren't going to say anything! You're going to give me every advantage to get at the truth. Then you go and push words in the mouth of your client. 'The gun your father gave you for your *protection.*'—All right, I'll tell you what *I'm* going to do. I'm going to take this woman to Los Angeles with me, and question her there."

"Going to arrest her?" Mason asked.

"If you want to force my hand, yes."

"All right," Mason said, "I'll force your hand."

"Very well," the deputy announced, "Mrs. Hardisty, you're under arrest. I warn you that anything you say may be used against you."

"Under arrest for what?" Mason demanded. "You can't arrest her without telling her the specific charge."

The deputy hesitated.

"Go on," Mason taunted. "If you're going to take her out of that room as being under arrest, you're going to arrest her on a specific charge. Otherwise she doesn't leave this house."

The officer hesitated another second or two, then blurted, "All right, I'll do it up brown. Mrs. Hardisty, I'm an officer of the law. I'm arresting you for the murder of your husband. As an officer of the law, I have reasonable ground to believe that you were guilty of that murder. Now you won't be permitted to talk with anyone. Get your things on. We're leaving for Los Angeles right now."

Mason said, "And, as this woman's attorney, I advise her not to answer any questions asked her by anyone unless those questions are asked in my presence."

The deputy said angrily, "I should have known better

than to have let you come along. I'll know better next time."

Mason smiled, "And if you'd tried to stop me from coming along you'd know better than to have tried *that* next time."

7

Mason stopped by the Kenvale Hotel to find Della Street waiting in the lobby.

"Find out about that cabin?" he asked.

"Yes. I went to the county assessor's office and got the thing definitely located."

"Just where?" Mason asked.

"It's in Los Angeles County, but as near as I could tell from making measurements on the map, the cabin is just about fourteen hundred feet from the county line."

"But the road to the cabin crosses the line into Kern County?"

"That's right. The private road to the cabin turns off just beyond the county line."

"How far beyond?"

"Not far—around two hundred feet."

Mason chuckled.

"What is it?" she asked.

Mason said, "If the murder was committed where the car was pushed over the grade, and the body was then brought back to the cabin, the murder was committed in Kern County. But if the murder was committed in the cabin, then, of course, it was committed in Los Angeles

County. Right now the officers may not know the answer to that."

"Isn't there some law that covers that, though?" Della Street asked suspiciously.

"Exactly," Mason said. "Section 782 of our Penal Code. . . . And *that's* going to make it nice."

"Come on, tightwad, loosen up."

"That section provides that when a murder is committed within five hundred yards of the boundary of two or more counties, the jurisdiction lies in either county."

"Then why the chuckle? In this case either county could take jurisdiction."

Mason said, "You'll see, if it works out—and I think it will."

"What happened out at the house?" she asked.

Mason ceased smiling.

"I sure led with my chin on that one. She was there."

"Milicent Hardisty?"

"Yes."

"But wasn't she suppoed to be there?"

"That's what the officers supposed. Blane told me she wasn't."

"Was Blane lying to you?"

"I don't know. I don't think so. It certainly made me feel as though someone had kicked me in the stomach when she opened the door. There I was, standing helplessly by, letting the officers get hold of my client before I'd had any chance to talk with her. . . . Has Adele Blane called you up yet?"

"No."

"She will. I want to see her. She may as well come home now. Tell her that when she calls—only to be certain to see me first."

Della glanced at him, said, "You sound almost as though you'd arranged her disappearance. . . . What did they do with Mrs. Hardisty?"

54

"Put her under arrest and they're going to bury her."

"What do you mean by that?"

"Ordinarily prisoners charged with murder are taken to the county jail, but if the authorities have an idea they can do more with a prisoner by taking him to some other jail, they do so. . . . You can see the situation with Milicent Hardisty. I told her not to answer questions. Perhaps she will. Perhaps she won't. In any event, they know I'm going to try to see her. It's a ten-to-one bet that instead of taking her to the Los Angeles jail where I can find her, they'll take her to some other town in the county and hold her there. By the time I finally locate her, they'll have had plenty of time to work on her. That's what is known as 'burying a prisoner.' "

"Isn't that unethical?"

Mason grinned. "There are no ethics when you're dealing with the police. Or I should say when the police are dealing with you. *You're* supposed to be bound by ethics. The police don't have ethics. They act on the assumption that they're *'getting the truth,'* whereas you are *'protecting a criminal.'* "

"That doesn't seem right," Della said.

"Of course, you have to admit this. The police *are* trying to solve crimes. They sincerely believe that everything they do has a tendency to uncover the truth, that anything they're stopped from doing is a monkey-wrench in the machinery. Therefore they look on all laws which are passed to protect the citizen as being obstacles thrown in front of the police. . . . Well, I suppose I've got to go start proceedings for a writ of *habeas corpus*. It'll take me two or three hours. You stay here and run things while I'm gone."

"What do you want me to do?"

Mason said, "Harley Raymand for one. Get him to go back to that cabin and look around."

"Why?"

"I'm not entirely satisfied with some things."

"What, for instance?"

"Evidently Jack Hardisty wore nose-pincher glasses. I saw the marks on his nose where the supports dug in."

"Well?"

"He didn't have his glasses on."

"Wasn't he partially undressed?"

"Yes."

"Men don't go to bed with their glasses on."

"I couldn't see them anywhere in the room."

"He probably put them in his coat pocket when he undressed."

"Perhaps—but other things indicate he didn't undress himself."

"What?"

"The shoes."

"What about the shoes?"

"The shoes," Mason said, "looked as though Hardisty had just stepped out of a shoeshining parlor."

"What's wrong with that?"

"If Harley Raymand and Adele Blane are telling the truth, Hardisty got out of his car and walked around among the pine needles. That would make the shoes pretty dusty, but there's something else about the shoes that bothers me."

"What?"

"I noticed that they were put under the bed with the toes pointing *toward* the bed."

"Well?"

Mason said, "Nine persons out of ten sitting on a bed and undressing will take off their shoes and put them down so the toes are pointing away from the bed; but if another person puts shoes down by a bed where a person is sleeping, he'll almost invariable point the toes *toward* the bed."

Della thought that over, then nodded thoughtful acquiescence.

"Now, then," Mason went on, "if you had noticed the bottom part of Jack Hardisty's trousers, you'd have observed that there was a little mud on them—a dried, reddish clay—not much, but enough to show. Now it hasn't rained here in Southern California for a month. Jack Hardisty would hardly have carried mud around on his trousers for a month. . . . I want to get Harley Raymand to explore around and see if he can find some place where a stream of water runs through reddish clay."

"But if he walked in the reddish clay, why didn't it stick to his shoes?"

"That's exactly it. He either took off his shoes and socks, and walked in there barefooted, or else cleaned his shoes afterwards."

"Good Heavens, why?"

Mason grinned and said, "Perhaps ninety thousand dollars in cash would be the answer."

"Oh, I see. . . . Do you want me to point that out to Mr. Raymand?"

"Definitely not."

"Anything else?"

"Yes. Tell Raymand to make a search for that clock, keep listening for the sound of ticking. If he gets his hands on the clock again, have him bring it to me at once."

"Okay," Della Street said, "I'll start Raymand out. Any—"

"Yes. Here's something I want you to do with Paul Drake. It's going to be tricky, but he can put it across."

"What?"

"Under that section of the penal code, the jurisdiction lies in either Kern County or Los Angeles County. Now, if Paul Drake could get some newspaper reporter

57

to put a bug in the ear of the district attorney of Kern County that this was going to be a spectacular case, with a chance for big notoriety and a possibility of political advancement for the district attorney who tries it—well, you know how it is. That's the sort of thing that prosecutors in small counties eat up."

"Then you want the case to be tried in Kern County?"

"No. I want each county to think the other is trying to steal the show."

"I'll tell Paul to fix it up. Anything else?"

"I think," Mason told her, "that will be enough."

8

Harley Raymand realized with some surprise that the events of the day had not dragged him down as much as he had anticipated. His sleep in the cool, crisp air at the mountain cabin had rested his nerves and given him the feeling that he was "over the hump."

The sheriff's office had been very thorough. The mattress and bedding had been removed from the bed and taken to Los Angeles for expert examination. Harley gathered there was quite a question in the minds of the authorities as to whether Hardisty had been shot while he was lying in the bed, or whether the body had been transferred to the bed within a short time after the murder had been committed. . . . And now Harley was working with definite objectives in mind: to find moist, reddish-brown clay—to find the clock—to locate the spade which had been in Hardisty's car, and, in general, to pick up any stray clues which might have been overlooked by the police—those things which a person actually living in a place might notice, but which would escape the attention of a more casual investigator.

Vincent Blane had asked him if it would make him nervous staying alone in a cabin where a murder had been committed. . . . Harley smiled every time he thought of that; he who had been trained to carry on while comrades were shot down all around him; he who had become so familiar with death that it had ceased to inspire him even with healthy respect, let alone fear, being afraid to sleep in a cabin simply because a man had been shot in it!

The rays of afternoon sunlight were once more slanting across from ridge to ridge while the valleys cradled purple shadows. Harley strolled across the pine-scented, sloping flat where the clock had been buried. Whoever had removed that clock had made a very cunning and thoroughly workmanlike job of replacing dirt in the hole, tamping it down, cleaning up each particle of surplus earth, and spreading moss and pine needles over the place.

Not only was there no sign of the clock, but Harley was forced to admit that if he, himself, had not seen the buried box at this particular place, he would have doubted the word of anyone who told him a clock had been buried there.

The moss and pine needles were a cushion under his feet.

The tall, straight trees caught the golden sunlight, cast long shadows. . . . Some sparkling object reflected the sun's rays with scintillating brilliance and a rim of color.

Harley moved over toward the rock outcropping, with the realization that the object reflecting the sun's rays must have come from a seam in the rock.

Upon approaching the rock, however, he could find nothing that could have caused the reflection. The seam in the rock held a threadlike line of pine needles which would furnish a background of dark green contrast to any metallic object which might have been there.

Puzzled, Harley retraced his steps to the point where he had first seen the shimmer of reflected sunlight, and moved back and forth, up and down, until suddenly he once more caught the glittering reflection. This time, he marked the place carefully and walked toward it without taking his eyes from it.

Just as he reached the rock, something urged him to turn.

Lola Strague was less than twenty feet behind him.

"Hello," she said with a little laugh, "what are *you* zig-zagging back and forth about?"

Slightly irritated, Harley said, "And may I ask what *you* were stalking?"

"Was I stalking?"

"You were very quiet."

"Perhaps your attention was concentrated on what you were doing, and you didn't hear me."

Harley became dignified. "Were you," he asked, "looking for me?"

"Not definitely."

"Then may I ask what you *were* looking for?"

She laughed. "I presume, when you come right down to it, I'm a trespasser, although the property lines aren't very clearly marked around here. No fences, or signs, you know. . . . And I found a gun here earlier in the day. That should give me the right to return."

"I'm not worried about the trespassing," he said, "but I had the distinct impression you were looking for something, and that you were being just a bit—well, furtive."

"Did you, indeed! That interests me a lot. Do you trust the impressions you form that way, or do you find they

60

are sometimes misleading? I'm collecting data for an article I intend to write on the subject."

He said, "I trust my impressions. My first impression was that you were looking for something, just as my present impression is that you are stalling around, trying to avoid answering my question until you can think up just the right answer."

She laughed. "I guess your impressions are all right, Mr. Raymand. I'll be fair with you. I was looking for the clock."

"And why so interested in *it?*"

"I don't know. I'm always interested in the mysterious, in those things that aren't explained. . . . And now, since I've answered your question, I'll ask you one. What are *you* looking for?"

"Health, rest, fresh air and relaxation," he said.

Her eyes were laughing at him. "Go on."

"*And* the clock," he admitted.

"And why were *you* so interested in the clock?"

"Because I have an idea the police are half convinced that I'm lying about it."

"You had a witness, didn't you?"

"Adele Blane, yes."

Lola Strague made her next question casual—perhaps just a little too casual. "Where is Adele Blane now?" she asked.

Harley frowned, said, "I presume she's trying to get in contact with Milicent—Mrs. Hardisty, you know. That's her sister."

"I see," Lola said, making the words sound quite unconvincing. "Wasn't she up here last night?"

"She was up here with me yesterday afternoon."

"And she came back afterwards?"

"I don't know. I went to the hotel and slept."

The tall, slender girl moved over to the outcropping, adjusting her pliable young body to the irregularities of the rock. Her eyes regarded Harley Raymand with disconcerting steadiness. "Are you going to join us up here, or are you just vacationing?"

"What do you mean?" he asked, managing to seat himself in such a position as to conceal the exact point in the rock seam from which he had caught the reflected light.

"Oh, you know. Are you going to live a leisurely life, or run in the breathless pursuit of success?"

"I don't know. Right now, I'm getting acquainted with myself, taking a breathing spell. I haven't blueprinted the future."

She picked up a little twig and traced aimless designs on the surface of the rock. "This war seems sort of a nightmare. It will pass, and people will wake up."

"To what?" Harley asked.

She looked up from her design tracing. "Sometimes," she admitted, "I'm afraid of that."

They were silent for a space of time, while Harley watched the creeping shadow of a pine limb move from her shoulder up to the lobe of her ear.

"Somehow," she said, "society got off on a wrong track. The thing people pursued as success wasn't success at all."

Harley kept silent, clothing himself in the luxury of lazy lethargy.

"Look at Mr. Blane," she went on. "He's an exponent of that system—driving himself. Now he's around fifty-five. He has high blood pressure, pouches under his eyes, a haunted expression. His motions are jerky and nervous. . . . You can't think that life was intended to be that way. He never relaxes, never takes a good long vacation; he has too many irons in the fire. And they say he isn't getting anywhere; that the income taxes are taking all he makes, and keeping his nose to the grindstone."

Harley felt that loyalty to Vincent Blane demanded speech. He aroused himself to say, "All right, let's look at Mr. Blane. I happen to know something about him. His parents died when he was a child. His first job paid him twelve dollars a week. He educated himself while he was working. He's responsible for two banks, one in Kenvale, one in Roxbury. He's put up a big department store. He gives employment to a large number of people. He built up the community."

"And what does it get him?" Lola Strague asked.

Harley thought that over, said, "If you want to look at it that way, what does it get *us?* He's a representative American, typical of the spirit of commercial progress which has changed this country from a colony to a nation."

"Are you," she asked abruptly, "going to work for him?"

"I don't know."

"Are you working for him now?"

"Is that—well, shall we say, pertinent?"

"You mean, is it any of my business?"

He shook his head. "I didn't express it that way."

"But that was what you meant?"

"No. I wondered if it might actually have some bearing."

"On what?"

"On—well, your attitude toward me."

Her eyes flashed quick interest, then were hastily averted as the end of the pine twig she was holding started scratching away at the rock again. "What were you doing out here?" she asked.

"When?"

"When I walked up just now."

"Looking at the place where the clock had been."

"And at something else on the rock," she said.

"Were you watching me?"

"Only just as I moved up. And when you sat down you acted as though you were concealing something."

He smiled at that, but said nothing.

"After all," she said, "I can sit here just as long as you can, if you're sitting on something to cover it up. It'll still be there when you get up."

"Of course, I could point out that you're trespassing."

"And eject me?"

"I might."

"In that event, you'd have to get up. I doubt if anyone has ever ejected a trespasser sitting down."

"And what makes you think I'm sitting here to conceal something?"

"I thought so when we started talking. I'm certain of it now."

"Why?"

"Otherwise, when I accused you of it, you'd have jumped up and looked around at the rock to see if there actually was anything to conceal."

"Perhaps I'm not as obvious as that."

"Perhaps."

"Very well," he said, "you win," and got up.

"What is it?" she asked.

"I don't know. Something was reflecting the light."

"There doesn't seem to be anything here."

"It must be a piece of glass. I can't understand anything else that—yes, there it is!"

"Looks like part of the lens from a pair of rimless glasses," she said, as Harley turned the curved piece of glass around in his fingers.

He nodded. "It must have fallen into these pine needles. They cushioned the shock and prevented it from breaking; also held it propped at just the right angle so it reflected the sun's rays just now."

"What do you make of it?" she asked.

Harley dropped the glass into his pocket. "I don't know. I'll have to think it over."

She laughed suddenly and said, "You're a cool one."

"Am I?"

"Yes."

He judged the time was ripe for a counter-offensive. "Why," he asked, "were you so upset when you learned Rodney Beaton was returning from town with Myrna Payson?"

Her face flamed into color. "That's an unfair question. You're insinuating that—"

"Yes?" Harley prompted as she ceased speaking abruptly.

She said, "It's a personal, impertinent and unfair question."

"You've been asking me questions," he said, "about my plans, and—"

"Simply being sociable," she interjected.

"And," Raymand said, smiling, "trying to find out something about my future moves and how long I'd be here. Hence, my question. Are you going to answer it?"

She caught her breath, preparatory to making some indignant comment, then seemed abruptly to change her mind. "Very well," she said with cold formality, "I will answer your question because apparently you think it's relevant and material. If you think I'm jealous, you're mistaken. I was merely piqued."

"There's a difference?" he asked.

"In my case, yes."

"And why were you piqued?"

"Because Rodney Beaton had stood me up. We had a date to go out and patrol the trails together."

"I'm afraid I don't understand."

She said, "Rodney is getting a collection of photographs of nocturnal animals. He has three or four cameras rigged with flashguns, and clamps them on tripods in strategic places on the trails. During the early part of the evenings he'll patrol the trails, finding the camera traps that have been touched off by passing animals. Then he'll put in fresh plates, reset the shutter, and put in a new flashbulb."

"And you accompany him?"

"At times."

"And last night he had given you some specific invitation?"

"Oh, it wasn't like that. It was just casual. He asked me if I was going to be doing anything, and I said no, and he said 'if you're around, we might take a look at the cameras,' and I told him I'd be glad to. That's what makes me angry. It wasn't a definite date—and he'd evidently forgotten all about it. If he'd made a definite date with me, and then broken it to go to town with that . . . that . . . with Mrs. Payson, I'd at least know where I stood. But it was casual and informal, and he simply forgot all about it. That puts me in the position of having to pretend that *I* forgot all about it, too. It's quite possible that Rodney will remember it later—and then it will be mutually embarrassing. And I think Mrs. Payson knew about it—and deliberately inveigled him into taking her to town. She's a widow, one of the—oh, let's not talk about her! Now then, that's the whole story. You see, it's a very commonplace affair. I think any young woman hates to be stood up. . . . But I don't want you to get the idea that I'm setting my cap for Mr. Rodney Beaton."

"Did I give you the impression that I thought that?"

She met his eyes fairly. "Yes," she said.

"While we're on the subject," he said, smiling, "since we've disposed of Rodney Beaton, what can you tell me about Myrna Payson?"

"Not much. She's a widow. She inherited some money. She's gone in for cattle ranching."

"Has a place up here?"

"She has a small ranch up here. She has two other ranches, and—well, *she* goes around with Rodney, taking care of the cameras quite frequently."

66

"Rodney seems to be very popular."

"He's a very interesting man, and—I don't know how I could describe it so you'll appreciate it, but there's a terrific wallop in this camera hunting."

"I don't get it."

"You set your camera, put in a flashbulb, string a black silk thread across the trail. If you're after animals the size of a coyote, you put it at a certain height. If you're looking for deer, you'll raise the thread. If you're after the smaller animals, you put it just an inch or two above the trail. Sometimes you string out three threads. You walk away, making a round of the other cameras, and come back at an interval of perhaps an hour. When you find the thread broken, the shutter tripped, and the flashbulb exploded, you know you've got a picture. Then you get down on your hands and knees and study the tracks in the trail to see what animal tripped the shutter. . . . Skunk pictures are usually cute. Deer pictures are hard to get, and quite frequently, deer photographed under those conditions seem angular and ungraceful. Foxes usually make beautiful pictures. Wildcats have a sinister look about them.

"Rod is a very expert photographer. He has infinite patience. He'll prospect for days to get just the right camera location—a smooth, fairly level stretch where there's no background to show—"

"Why no background?" Harley interrupted.

"Because Rod only wants the animal against a dead black background. He uses a small flashbulb and a wide-open lens. He says most flashlight pictures give an effect of unreality because they show garish foreground and black—but you must get Rod to show you his collection. It's wonderful."

"Does Mr. Beaton develop the films here?"

"Oh yes, he has a little darkroom in the cellar of his cabin. We go down there when we get back from our patrol and develop the films that have been exposed. That's when it gets exciting, seeing what you've got on the film, whether it's a good picture, whether the animal was facing the camera or facing away from the camera, or just trotting along the trail when it set off the flash-bulb."

"Ever get pictures of human beings?" Raymand asked.

"No, silly, of course not."

"What's to prevent someone walking along a trail and blundering into one of those camera traps?"

"Why—nothing, I guess, except that no one ever has done it so far. There's no reason for people to go prowling around these hills at night."

"And Myrna Payson takes an interest in night photography?"

Lola Strague became suddenly economical of words. "Yes."

"And there is a certain element of rivalry?"

"No."

"But you and Myrna Payson aren't particularly intimate?"

"I think I can settle that very quickly, Mr. Raymand. It's absolutely none of your business, but we're *quite* friendly. Up here, we all try to get along with one another, be friends, and—mind our own business."

"Ouch!"

"You asked for it."

"I did, indeed. What's more, I'm going to ask for more from time to time."

"If your questions are frank, you'll have to pardon me if my answers are also frank."

"Just so I get the information," Raymand grinned, "I don't care what sort of a verbal package it's wrapped in."

"I see. And precisely what information are you angling for?"

68

"I want to know why a good-looking young woman like Myrna Payson should be marooned up here—"

"She came up here a few weeks ago to look over her property. She intended to stay two days. It was just a trip of inspection."

"And she met Rodney Beaton?"

"Yes."

"And she has now been here for some several weeks, you say?"

"Yes."

"Then it took longer for her to investigate—"

"I don't know," Lola Strague interrupted irritably. "I'm really utterly incapable of reading Mrs. Payson's mind. I don't know what your object is, Mr. Raymand, but if you're up here trying to play detective, and are starting on the surmise that Myrna and I are engaged in some sort of a struggle for the affections or companionship of Rodney Beaton, you're . . . you're all wet. And now, if you'll pardon me, I'll be on my way. . . . Unless there are further questions?" Her manner was one of cold anger.

Harley said, "I'm simply trying to get the picture in focus in my mind. I—" He broke off to listen. "A car coming," he said.

She had caught the sound almost at the same time he had. They stood there wordlessly, waiting for the car to make its appearance, both yielding to a common curiosity, yet maintaining their dignified hostility.

Harley Raymand was the first to recognize the man who drove the car up out of the shadow-filled canyon to the gentle slope in front of the cabin. "It's Perry Mason, the lawyer," he said.

Mason saw them standing there, and swerved the car over to the side of the road, shut off the motor and came walking across to join them.

69

"Hello," he said. "You look very serious, as though you were engaged in a council of war."

"Or an altercation," Lola Strague said with a smile.

"Tell me, what have they done with Mrs. Hardisty?" Harley Raymand asked.

"I've got a writ of *habeas corpus* for her. They're going to have to bring her out into the open now. They've had her buried in some outlying town. . . . Were you people looking for something?"

"I came out here looking for the clock," Harley said.

"Find anything?"

"Not a sign. I've listened at various places—holding my ear to the ground. Can't hear a thing."

"You could hear it ticking fairly plainly when you first discovered it?"

"Yes. The sound seemed to carry well through the ground. It was quite audible."

Lola Strague regarded Harley Raymand with amused eyes. "Well," she asked, "are you going to tell him?"

Raymand reached his hand in his pocket. "While I was looking for the clock," he said, "I found a piece of glass. It looks as though it had been broken from a spectacle."

Mason took the piece of glass in his fingers, turned it around thoughtfully, said, "Just where was this, Raymand?"

Harley showed him.

Mason started looking along the needle-filled seam in the rock. "We should be able to find the rest of this. This is only about a half of one lens."

They searched the little fold in the rock carefully. Then Mason gave his attention to the surrounding ground. "That's mighty peculiar," he said. "Suppose a pair of spectacles were thrown against that rock and cracked into pieces. You'd naturally expect to find little pieces of glass around here on the ground. There doesn't seem to be a sign of anything, not even—wait a minute. What's this?"

70

He crawled forward on his hands and knees, picked up a wedge-shaped sliver of glass. "Looks as though this is also from a broken spectacle lens," Mason said. "And that seems to be the only other piece that's anywhere around here."

"What should I do with this piece that I've found?" Harley Raymand asked him. "Do you think I should report it?"

"I think it would be a good idea."

"To the sheriff's office?"

"Yes. Jameson, the resident deputy, is a pretty decent sort. You might get in touch with him. You can tell him about the piece you found. *I'll* tell him about the one I found."

Lola Strague smiled. "Much as I would like to hang around and wear my welcome out, I think I'd better be getting back. And, since I didn't find anything, *I* won't say anything to anyone."

Mason watched her walking down the trail, a slight smile twinkling at his eye corners. Then he turned to Harley Raymand, said, "I want to look around a little, and I'd better do it before sundown. . . . Where do cars customarily park up here?"

"Just about any place, I believe," Raymand replied. "I'm a little out of touch with things, but before I left, and when they'd have parties up here, people parked their cars wherever they found shade. There's eighty acres in the tract, which makes for quite a bit of individuality in parking automobiles."

Mason digested that information. "When I was here this morning, I noticed the deputy sheriff's car was parked under that tree. Did it stay in that one place?"

"Yes. Later on, when the Los Angeles men arrived during the first part of the afternoon and took the body away, they parked their cars right close to the porch on that side."

71

Mason strolled over to look at the tracks along the road, then walked leisurely to the back of the cabin. "This seems to be a fairly level place—"

"It's reserved for barbecues," Raymand said. "At least it was the last time I was a regular visitor here."

"Nevertheless," Mason observed, "a car seems to have swung around here, a car which left very distinct tire prints."

"That's right," Raymand agreed. "Those prints of two wheels certainly are distinct."

"The rear wheels," Mason pointed out. "You can see where they crossed over the tracks of the other wheels. . . . You don't know when those tracks were made, do you, Raymand?"

"No sir, I don't. I got up here quite a bit after dark last night, and—wait a minute. I know they *weren't* here yesterday afternoon, because I walked around back of the house to go to the spring. I'm quite certain I'd have noticed it if these car tracks had been here then."

Mason half closed his eyes in thoughtful contemplation. "Oh well, I guess the police have covered the ground. . . . Just ran by to see how you were making it, Raymand. I'll be at the hotel in case anything turns up."

9

Myrna Payson's ranch was some two miles beyond the point where the road turned off to the Blane cabin. Here the country changed to a rolling plateau, with little tree-filled valleys and several small lakes. In the distance, the peaks of mountains that bordered the plateau lifted crests that were some eight thousand feet above sea level.

Up here on the plateau, away from the shadows of the mountains, there was still enough sunlight, when Mason turned his car into the gate marked *"M Bar P,"* to turn the winding graveled road to a ribbon of reddish gold. An old-fashioned picket fence cast long, barred shadows. A sagging gate that hung disconsolately from one hinge reminded Mason somehow of a weary pack horse standing with its weight on three legs.

The house was a roomy, old-fashioned structure, weathered and paintless.

Mason parked his car, climbed three steps to a somewhat rickety porch, and, seeing no doorbell, knocked loudly.

He heard motion on the inside. Then the door was opened, and an attractive woman in the early thirties was sizing him up with curious eyes.

"Miss Payson?" Mason asked.

"Mrs. Payson. I'm a widow," she corrected. "Won't you come in?"

She had taken care of her figure, her skin, her hands and her dark hair. Her nose was perhaps a bit too upturned. Her mouth required makeup to keep the lips from seeming a shade too full. Her eyes looked out on life with a quizzical, slightly humorous expression, and she was quite evidently interested in people and things.

It was, Mason decided as he accepted her invitation and entered the house, an interest which would make this woman very fascinating. This was not the eager curiosity of the youngster, nor the exploitation of the adventuress, but rather the appraisal of one who has acquired a perspective, has lost all fear that events may get out of hand, and is quite frankly curious to see what new experiences life has to offer.

Mason said, "Aren't you a little afraid, being out here alone like this?"

"Of what?"

"Of strangers."

She laughed. "I don't think I've ever been afraid of anything or anyone in my life. . . . And I'm not alone."

"No?"

She shook her head. "There's a bunkhouse out here about fifty yards. I have three of the toughest bow-legged cowpunchers you ever saw. And you have, perhaps, overlooked the dog under the table."

Mason took a second look. What was apparently a patch of black shadows proved on closer inspection to be a shaggy substance that was taking in everything that was happening with watchful, unwinking eyes.

Mason laughed. "I will amend my statement about your being alone."

" 'Spooks' doesn't look formidable," she said, "but he's a living example of still water running deep. He never growls, never barks, but believe me, Mr. Mason, I have only to give him a signal and he'd come out of there like a steel spring."

"You know who I am, then?" Mason asked.

"Yes. I've seen your photograph in the papers, had you pointed out to me once or twice in night clubs. . . . I presume you want to ask me about what I saw when Rod and I went to town last night."

Mason nodded.

She smiled. "I'm afraid it won't do any good to ask."

"Why not?"

"In the first place," she said, slowly and distinctly, "I sympathize with that woman. I sympathize with her very, very much. In the second place, I wasn't interested in what she had in her hand. I was fascinated by what I saw on her face."

"What *did* you see on her face?" Mason asked.

74

She smiled. "And I know enough to realize that's not proper evidence, Mr. Mason. I don't think a court would let me testify to that, would it? Doesn't it call that opinion evidence, or a conclusion, or something of the sort?"

Mason smiled. "You're not in court, and I am very much interested in what you saw on her face. I don't know but what I'd be even more interested in that than in what she had in her hand."

Myrna Payson narrowed her eyes, as though trying to recall some vague memory into sharp focus. Abruptly she said, "But I haven't offered you a drink. How inhospitable of me!"

"No drink," Mason said, "not now, thanks. I'm very much interested in what you saw in Milicent Hardisty's face."

"Or a cigarette?"

"I have my own, thank you."

"Well now, let's see," Mrs. Payson said thoughtfully, "just how I can describe it. . . . It was a fascinating expression, the expression of a woman who has found herself, who has reached a decision and made a renunciation."

"That sounds rather definite and deliberate."

"Well?"

"The story, as I gathered it, is that Mrs. Hardisty was completely hysterical and emotionally upset."

Mrs. Payson shook her head. "Definitely not."

"You're certain?"

"Well, of course, Mr. Mason, when it comes to reading facial expressions, we all have our own ideas, but I've been interested in faces and in emotions. I have a very definite idea about Mrs. Hardisty from what I saw. And it's not anything I'm going to tell in court."

"Could you tell me?" Mason asked.

"You are acting as her lawyer?"

"Yes."

75

Mrs. Payson thought for a moment, then said, "Yes, I think I could tell you—if there were any reason why I should."

"There is," Mason assured her. "The authorities have buried Mrs. Hardisty. I can't get in touch with her. I'm called on to defend her for murder."

Mrs. Payson said, "Well, you'll laugh at me when I've told you, Mr. Mason."

"Why?"

"Because you'll say it's impossible for a person to learn so much of another's problems and decisions by a fleeting glimpse of a facial expression."

"I'll promise not to laugh," Mason said. "I may smile, I may doubt, I may question—but I won't laugh."

"On the strength of that promise, I'll tell you about Mrs. Hardisty. She had the expression of a woman waking up, of a woman who has definitely reached a decision, a decision to put something old out of her life and to go on with something new. I've seen that same expression two or three times before. I—I went through that experience myself once. I know what it's like."

"Go ahead," Mason said, as she hesitated.

She said, "Mr. Mason, I'll tell you something you can't use as evidence. It isn't worth a snap of your fingers anywhere. If you tell it to anyone, they'll laugh at you, but you can take it from a woman who knows her way around that Milicent Hardisty went out there to kill her husband. She went out with the deliberate intention of murdering him. Probably not because of the hurt he had inflicted on her, but because of the hurt he had inflicted on someone else. She came within an ace of killing him. Perhaps she even fired a shot and it missed. And then suddenly she realized the full potential effect of what she had almost done, realized what the gun she held in her hand really was. It ceased to be a mere means by which she could remove Jack Hardisty from her life forever, but became

76

the key which fitted the door of a prison cell. It became the symbol of a bondage to the law, something that would chain her to a cell until she was an old woman, until love had left her life forever. And she had this sudden revulsion of feeling, and wanted to get rid of that gun. She had a horror of it. She wanted to throw it so far she'd never see it again. And then she was going to the man she loved. And, regardless of consequences, regardless of gossip, regardless of conventions, she was going to live her life with that man. . . . Now, go ahead and laugh, Mr. Mason."

"I'm not laughing, not even smiling."

"And that," Mrs. Payson announced, "is all I know."

"That is what you would call the result of a woman's intuition?"

"That is what *I* would call applied psychology, the knowledge of character one gets when one has lived and gone through a lot—and I have."

Mason couldn't resist asking one more question. "How about Miss Strague?" he asked.

"What about her?"

"What do you deduce from *her* expressions?"

Mrs. Payson laughed. "Would that help you to clear Mrs. Hardisty?"

"It might."

Mrs. Payson said, "Lola Strague is a delightful girl. She's fresh, sweet, and she's spoiled. She waits on her brother hand and foot, but her brother idolizes the ground she walks on, and watches over her.

"She thinks I'm an adventuress; she's in love with Rodney Beaton; she thinks I have designs on him. She's somewhat amateurish in her little jealousies, and just a little hypocritical. She gets jealous, but she won't admit it, even to herself. She tries to rise above all the petty emotions. She pretends to herself that she's done so. And when she puts on that particular mask, she makes me terribly ill, because then she's being a damned little hypo-crite. But, in her inexperienced way, she's a very nice little girl. . . . However, I don't think she's the sort that Rodney Beaton would marry."

"And how," Mason asked, "do you feel toward Rodney Beaton?"

She looked him frankly in the eyes and laughed at him.

"Well, now let's see," Mason said. "What else can I ask you?"

"You seem to have taken rather a wide latitude."

"I've asked you just about everything I could think of. Could you swear that Mrs. Hardisty tossed the gun down the barranca?"

"I couldn't swear that she tossed anything down a bar-ranca. I think I saw her arm move. I couldn't swear to it. I don't know what was in her hand. I was watching her face. I tell you I was completely and utterly fascinated with her face."

"How about Burt Strague?" Mason asked.

"What about him?"

"What do you think of him?"

She hesitated a moment, then slowly shook her head.

"Not going to answer that one?" Mason asked.

"Not all of it," she said. "There's someting about Burt Strague that just doesn't fit into the picture. He has a sister complex. He's intensely loyal, emotionally unstable; he has a swift, devastating temper; he's un-doubtedly just what he says he is, and yet—and yet, there's something about him that—"

"Doesn't ring true?" Mason asked, as she hesitated, groping for words with which to express the idea.

"It isn't that," she said. "There's something about him —something that he's afraid of, something that his sister is afraid of, something they're fighting, some very dark chapter in his life."

"What makes you think that?"

"The way he's always watching himself, as though some careless word might betray something that must be kept secret at all costs. . . . There, I've told you more than I intended to tell you, and I presume you know why."

"Why?"

"Because I want to help Mrs. Hardisty. I wish all women could realize how much better it is to write off their emotional liabilities and turn to the future while there still *is* a future. Time slips through one's fingers so very imperceptibly, Mr. Mason, that it's tragic. When one is seventeen, twenty is getting old. When one is in the twenties, the thirties seems positively doddering, terribly distant. And the woman in the forties has to conceal her emotions; otherwise people laugh at her. . . . And there's a peculiar shifting viewpoint. When one is in the thirties, one looks at the thirties as being just the prime of life; when one's in the forties, one looks at the thirties with a feeling that they're still a little callow. Time is a clever robber."

"How does a woman of forty look to a man of forty?" Mason asked.

Mrs. Payson smiled. "She doesn't have a chance. A man of forty considers himself in the prime of life and starts ogling girls in the twenties. He reasons that other men of forty may be a little passé, but not him. He's 'exceptionally well preserved.' He's a man who 'looks ten years younger.' "

Mason grinned at her. "Well, how about the men in the sixties and seventies?" he asked.

Mrs. Payson reached for a cigarette. "I think," she announced laughing, "that you've got something there."

10

At the hotel Mason found Della Street waiting in the lobby.

"Hello," she exclaimed. "I'm starved! *What* do we do about it?"

"We eat," Mason proclaimed.

"That's swell. Paul Drake's here."

"Where?"

"Up in his room. They gave him a room next to yours, with a communicating door. . . . They say the hotel dining room is a fine place to eat, one of the best in the city."

"We can eat," Mason said, "on one condition."

"What's that?"

"That Jack Hardisty was killed before seven o'clock last night."

"But that's just the time Milicent was up there. You don't want the murder to have been committed while she was there, do you?"

"If it was," Mason said, "it's unfortunate, but there's nothing I can do. If it was committed later, it's also unfortunate, but there's a lot I'm going to have to do."

"What?"

"For one thing, I've got to take a chance—that the person to whom Milicent would turn when she was in desperate trouble, in whom she'd have utter and complete confidence, and who had recently been able to put two brand-new tires on his automobile, would be the family physician."

Della Street thought that over, said, "It sounds logical."

"Okay. Go telephone Vincent Blane. Make your question sound just as casual as possible. Ask him what physician in Roxbury could give us a certificate that Milicent is in a precarious nervous condition due to the strain of her domestic relations."

"Then what?" she asked.

"That's all. Just note the name of the doctor. Then come up to Paul Drake's room. . . . Is the local evening paper out?"

"Yes."

"Anything in it about Milicent?"

"Not a line. They haven't released a bit of information about the arrest."

"The story of the murder is in there?"

"Oh yes. Not a great amount of information, just the statement expanded and amplified and rehashed—the way they do with news nowadays."

"All right. Go put through that call. I'll run up to see Paul."

"Do you want me to telephone from my room or from the lobby?"

"Booth in the lobby. The girl at the switchboard might be curious."

Della Street nodded, moved over toward the telephone booth. Mason went up in the elevator, unlocked the door of his own room, crossed through the communicating door to the adjoining room, and found Paul Drake standing in front of the mirror just finishing shaving with an electric razor.

"Hello, Perry," Drake said, disconnecting the razor and splashing shaving lotion on his face. "What's news?"

"That's what I came up to find out."

Drake put on his shirt and knotted his necktie.

"Well?" Mason asked.

Drake said nothing for the moment, concentrating his attention on getting his tie knotted just right. He was tall, limber, loose-jointed, and his appearance was utterly at variance with the popular conception of what a detective should be. In repose, his face held a lugubrious lack of interest; his eyes, which missed nothing, seemed to be completely oblivious of what was taking place about him. Behind this mask a logical mind worked with mathematical certainty and ball-bearing speed.

"What's the matter?"

"That Milicent girl."

"What about her?"

"You told me to find her, that I could pass up all the tips that she'd be easy to find. You gave me a pretty broad hint that I'd hear she was in her house but that that was just a gag you'd thought up to hand to the cops. Well, I put a flock of men——"

"I know," Mason interrupted, "I was fooled worse than you were."

Drake looked at him, trying to read more meaning into the lawyer's words. "It *wasn't* a stall you'd thought up for the police?"

Mason merely smiled.

"It floored me," Drake went on. "I was looking in all the hide-out places, and here she was at her father's house, tucked safely in bed, with a housekeeper answering all inquiries by saying, 'Yes, she's here, but she can't be disturbed.'"

"And there she was," Mason said.

"Exactly."

"Well, Paul, you've crabbed from time to time that I gave you jobs that were too tough. This was an easy one. All you had to do to locate her was phone her father's house."

Drake said, "Don't give me any more of those 'easy' ones or I'll go nuts."

"What else have you done?" Mason asked.

"Think I've got some place with the Kern County idea. The D.A. over there could use a little publicity."

"What's he doing?"

"Nothing violent yet, but he's sitting up and taking interest. If we could dig up a spectacular angle on the case, I think he'd fall for it. . . . You know, the newspapers like to get an interesting handle they can tack onto a murder—the Tiger Woman Case, the White Flash Case, the Snake-Eyes Murder. . . . Thought maybe you could work out something with that buried clock that would be an angle. Then the city newspapers would go to town on it, and when that happened I think Kern County would move in."

"What time was the murder committed?" Mason asked.

"Can't tell you that yet," Drake said. "I've got a man working on that angle."

Mason frowned. "The autopsy surgeon must have made at least a preliminary report."

Drake said, "That's the queer part of it. They're not releasing anything based on a preliminary report. Makes it seem there's something in the case that doesn't fit."

Mason nodded.

Drake said, "You don't seem very enthusiastic about that, Perry."

"I'm always suspicious of the things in cases that don't fit," Mason said. "I've seen too many lawyers grab hold of some isolated fact that didn't fit and brandish it around in front of a jury. Then something would click and that particular fact fitted into a particular interpretation that hung the client."

When Drake was thinking, he always sought for complete bodily relaxation, propping himself against something or sprawling all over a chair. Now he placed an elbow on the back of a chair, then after a moment, sidled around so that he was sitting on the rounded overstuffed arm, his elbow resting against the back, his hand propping up his chin. "What I'm afraid of is that the D.A.'s office isn't going to pay any attention to that buried clock. They think it's a fairy story. If they play it down the newspapers won't play it up."

Mason said, "I can *almost* give them a theory on that clock, Paul."

Drake said, "Give me a theory that will hold water, and I'll show you some action."

"Ever hear of sidereal time, Paul?"

"What's sidereal time?"

"Star time."

"Are you kidding me?"

"No."

"Why is star time different from sun time?"

"Because the stars gain a day on the sun every year."

"I don't get you."

"The earth makes a big circle around the sun and returns to the place where it started once each year. The effect of that circle is to make the stars rise about two hours earlier every month, or a total gain of twenty-four hours in the twelve months. By keeping clocks that run about four minutes fast every day, astronomers can keep star time instead of sun time.

"Time really is nothing but a huge circle. You divide a circle of three hundred and sixty degrees into twenty-four hours, and you get fifteen degrees of arc that is the equivalent of each hour."

"You're getting too complicated for me," Drake said. "I don't get it."

Mason said, "It's simple enough, once you get the idea. What I'm trying to point out is that by using sidereal time, astronomers know the exact position of any given star at any given moment."

"How?"

"Well, they give each star a certain time position in the heavens, which is known as its 'right ascension.' Then, by knowing the right ascension, looking at a clock and getting the sidereal time, they can know the exact position of the star. That's the way they work the astronomical telescopes. They get the position of the star at a given moment, turn the telescope so that the angle is exactly right, set it for latitude on another graduated circle known as the star's *declination*,' look in the finder telescope—and there's the star."

"All right," Drake grinned, "there's the star—so what?"

Mason said, "So, it's a newspaper headline."

Drake thought that over. "I believe you've got something there, Perry—if we could make it stick. What makes you think *this* clock was geared according to this sidereal time you're talking about?"

Mason said, "Look at it this way, Paul. Twice during the year, sidereal time must agree with civil time—once when it hits it right on the nose, and again when it's gained twelve hours, which would have the effect, on a twelve-hour clock, of—"

"Yes, yes, I know," Drake said. "I can figure that out."

"One of these times when sidereal time agrees with civil or sun time, is at the time of the equinox on September twenty-third."

"And then the clock goes on gaining four minutes a day?" Drake asked.

"That's right."

"But this clock was twenty-five minutes *slow*."

"Thirty-five minutes fast," Mason said, smiling.

"I don't get you."

"You've forgotten that our time has been advanced an hour. Therefore, our war time is an hour ahead of

85

sun time, so that a clock that was twenty-five minutes slow on our war time would be thirty-five minutes fast on our sun time. . . . That gives us something to think about."

"Something to think about is right," Drake said. "If we can tie this murder in with astrology, or even astronomy, we'll give it so much notoriety the district attorney of Kern County—will grab at it like a hungry dog grabbing a bone."

Mason said, "Well, it's an angle to think over. All it is, is just a publicity gag for the newspapers, but it'll give them a handle—a tag line."

"I'll say it will," Drake said. "When can I go to town with that, Perry?"

"Almost any time."

Della Street's knock sounded on the door. "Everybody decent?" she called.

"Come on in, Della."

Della Street entered, grinned a salutation at the detective, and walked across to slip a folded piece of paper into Mason's hand.

Drake, whose eyes apparently were centered with fixed interest on some object at the far end of the room, said, "You're ruining that girl, Perry."

"How so?"

"It's the legal training. She's getting so she doesn't trust anyone. You tell her to get some information, and she knows you'll be in here talking with me, so she writes it out on a piece of paper and slips it to you."

Mason laughed, said, "She knows you have a one-track mind, Paul. She doesn't want to distract it." He unfolded the paper.

Della Street had written merely a name on a sheet of paper torn from her notebook. *"Dr. Jefferson Macon, Roxbury."*

Drake said, "There's a story going around that Hardisty had been dipping into funds at the bank. I suppose you're not going to tell me about that. You—"

The telephone rang.

Drake said, "This is probably one of the boys with a report." He picked up the receiver, placed it to his ear, said, "Hello," and then let his face become a mask while he digested the information which was distinguishable to the other occupants of the room only as harsh, metallic noises emanating from time to time from the receiver.

"You're certain?" Drake asked at length. Then, evidently being assured that there was no doubt about the matter, added, "Stay where you are. I may call you back in about five minutes. I'll want to think this over."

He hung up the receiver, turned to Mason and said, "The report of the autopsy surgeon shows Jack Hardisty was killed sometime after seven o'clock, probably around nine o'clock. The time limits are fixed as being between seven o'clock and ten-thirty."

Mason pushed his hands down deep in his trousers pockets, studied the pattern on the faded hotel carpet intently, suddenly snapped a question at the detective. "Was the fatal bullet in the body, Paul?"

The question jarred expression into Drake's face, shattering the mask of wooden-faced disinterest with which the detective customarily masked his thoughts. "Perry, what the devil put that idea in your mind?"

"Was it?" Mason asked.

"No," Drake said. "That's the thing the autopsy surgeon can't figure. That's one of the reasons he held up his report until he'd made a double check. The man was undoubtedly killed with a bullet, probably from a thirty-eight caliber weapon. The bullet didn't go clean through the body—*and the bullet isn't there!*"

Mason nodded slowly, thoughtfully digesting that information.

"You don't seem surprised," Drake said.

"What do you want me to do—throw up my hands and say 'my, my'?"

Drake said, "Bunk! You can't fool me, Perry. You anticipated that very thing."

"What makes you think so?"

"Your question."

"It was just a question."

"And I'll bet this is the only murder case in which you ever asked it."

Mason said nothing.

"Well," Drake told him, "in any event that lets Milicent out."

"What does?"

"The fact that the murder took place after she left the cabin."

Mason shook his head slowly. "No, Paul, it doesn't let her out; it drags her in. I'm sorry, but I'm having to pass up dinner. Take Della—on the expense account."

Drake said, "There are times, Perry, when you get some very commendable ideas."

"Do I know where I can reach you, in case anything turns up?" Della Street asked Perry Mason.

He nodded.

"Where?"

The lawyer merely smiled.

Della said, "I get you."

"And I *don't*," the detective protested.

Della Street placed her fingers on his arm. "Never mind, Paul. We're going to dinner—on the expense account. . . . Do your dinners include cocktails, Paul?"

"They always have when they've been on an expense account," Drake said, "although Perry probably doesn't know it."

Mason grinned, took the sliver of glass from his pocket.

"A piece of a spectacle lens, Paul," he said, handing the sliver to the detective.

Drake turned it over in his fingers. "What about it?"

Mason started for the door. "That's what I'm paying you for, Paul."

11

Roxbury's main street seemed strangely surreptitious with its unlighted neon signs, its shielded illumination, making the figures of pedestrians appear vague, shadowy and unreal.

Perry Mason, driving slowly along, counted the intersections to find the cross street that he wanted, turned abruptly to the right, ran his car for a block and a half, and stopped in front of a white stucco, red tile, pretentious house. The sign on the lawn which said "DR. JEFFERSON MACON" was hardly visible, now that the street lights had been extinguished.

Mason climbed a flight of short steps, found a bell button, and pushed it. A broad-beamed middle-aged woman with unsmiling countenance opened the door and said, "The doctor's evening hours are nine to ten."

Mason said, "I want to see him upon an urgent private matter."

"Do you have a card?"

Mason said impatiently, "Tell him Perry Mason, a lawyer, would like to see him at once."

The woman said, "Wait here, please," turned on her heel and marched with slow, deliberate steps down a corridor, pushed open a door and banged it shut behind her, the explosive sound of the closing door conveying definite disapproval.

Mason had been standing for almost a minute when she returned, coming toward him with the same slow, deliberate steps—heavy-footed, wooden-faced.

She waited until she had assumed exactly the same position which she had been in when Mason first saw her—evidently her answering-the-door stance. "The doctor will see you."

Mason followed her back down the corridor, through the door and into a small, book-lined room, near the center of which, in a huge black leather chair, Dr. Jefferson Macon was stretched out, completely relaxed.

"Good evening," he said. "Please be seated. Pardon me for not getting up. The exigencies of my profession are such that I must ruin my own health safeguarding the health of others. If I had a patient who lived the life I do, I'd say he was committing suicide. As it is, I have been forced to make it a rule to relax for half an hour after each meal. . . . Kindly state what it is you wish. Be brief. Don't be disappointed if I show no reaction whatever. I'm training myself to relax completely and shut out all extraneous affairs."

Mason said, "That's fine. Go ahead and relax all you want. Did Milicent Hardisty spend all the night here last night, or just part of it?"

Dr. Macon jerked himself into a rigid sitting posture. "What—*what's that?*"

He was, Mason saw, a man approaching fifty, firm-fleshed, steady-eyed, slender. Yet there was in the man's face that grayish look of fatigue which comes to those who are near the point of physical exhaustion from the strain of overwork.

Mason said, "I wanted to know whether Milicent Hardisty spent the entire night here or only part of it."

"That's presumptuous. That's a dastardly insinuation! That—"

"Can you answer the question?" Mason interrupted.

"Yes, of course. I can answer it."

"Then what's the answer?"

"I see no reason for giving you any answer."

Mason said, "She's been arrested."

"Milicent—arrested? You mean the authorities think— why, that's shocking!"

"You knew nothing of it?" Mason asked.

"I certainly did not. I had no idea the police would be so stupid as to do anything of the sort."

Mason said, "There's some circumstantial evidence against her."

"Then the evidence has been misinterpreted."

"Go right ahead," Mason said, motioning toward the deep cushions of the chair. "Lie right back and relax. I'll just ask questions. You keep on relaxing."

Dr. Macon continued to sit bolt upright.

Mason said, "Everyone's acted on the assumption that Hardisty's death occurred early in the evening. Quite possibly ten or fifteen minutes before deep dusk. A report's just come in from the autopsy surgeon. They held it up until they could make a double check, because it didn't agree with what the police thought were the facts."

Dr. Macon stroked the tips of his fingers across his cheek. "May I ask what the report indicated?"

"Death between seven and ten-thirty," Mason said. "Probably, around nine."

"Did I understand you to say probably around nine o'clock?"

"Yes."

"Then that—then Milicent couldn't possibly have been connected with it."

"Why?"

91

"She was . . . she was home at that time, wasn't she?"

"How do you know?"

Dr. Macon caught himself quickly and said, "I don't. I was only asking."

"What time were you up there?"

"Where?"

"Up at the Blane cabin."

"You mean that *I* went up there?"

Mason nodded.

Dr. Macon said somewhat scornfully, "I'm afraid I don't appreciate your connection with the case, Mr. Mason. I know who are are, of course. I would like to meet you under more favorable—and I may say, more friendly—circumstances; but I am afraid you are definitely barking up the wrong tree. I am, of course, enough of a psychologist to appreciate the technique of a cross-examination in which startling questions are propounded without warning to an unsuspecting witness and—"

Mason interrupted him to say, apparently without feeling, "I may be mistaken."

"I'm glad to hear you say so."

"Whether I am or not," Mason said, "depends on the tires on your automobile."

"What do you mean?"

"An automobile left tracks up at the Blane cabin. I don't think the significance of those tracks has occurred to the police—as yet. The Los Angeles deputies took it for granted the tracks were made by the local authorities. It evidently hasn't occurred to the local authorities to check up on them."

"What about them?"

"They were the tracks of *new* tires."

"What if they were?"

Mason smiled. "Perhaps in your position, Doctor, you haven't as yet appreciated the seriousness of tire rationing, and therefore have dismissed it from your mind."

"I'm afraid I don't—"

"Oh, yes you do. You're stalling for time, Doctor. You recently had two new tires put on the back wheels of your automobile. Undoubtedly you had to get those tires through the tire rationing board. There's a complete record of installation, application for purchase, and all that. As soon as I saw the *new* tire marks, it occurred to me that I was dealing with a police car. When I found out it couldn't have been a police car, I simply started running down the other angles. It isn't everyone who could possibly have *two brand-new tires* on his automobile, you know."

"And that investigation brought you to me?"

Mason nodded.

"I suppose you realize," Dr. Macon said, with frigid formality, "that you are making a most serious charge."

"I haven't made any charge yet but I'm going to make one in a minute—as soon as you quit stalling around."

"Really, Mr. Mason, I think this is uncalled for."

"So do I. I'm trying to help my client."

"And who is your client, may I ask?"

"Milicent Hardisty."

"She has retained you?"

"Her father did."

"She is—you say she is charged with—"

"Murder."

"I can't believe it possible."

Mason looked at his watch. "You've got to start seeing people at nine o'clock, Doctor. Time's limited. I took a short cut getting here. I saw the tracks of two new tires and jumped at conclusions. The officers will go at it more methodically. They can't afford to play hunches. They'll probably make a cast of the tire marks, check with the tire rationing board on all permits for new tires, check with dealers for sales, and eventually they'll get here. I'm simply leading the procession."

93

Dr. Macon shifted his position uneasily. "I take it that anything I may say to you will be entirely confidential, Counselor."

"Guess again."

"You mean it won't?"

"That's right."

"But I thought you said you were representing Milicent Hardisty."

"I am."

"I—"

"I'm representing her, and no one else. Anything *she* tells me is confidential; anything *you* tell me is something I use or don't use, depending on *her* best interests."

"If she has an alibi for—well, from seven o'clock on until midnight, that would absolve her from any connection with the crime?"

"Probably."

"I—" Dr. Macon's voice dissolved into a somewhat dubious silence.

"Make up your mind," Mason said.

Dr. Macon said, "I want to tell you a little story."

"I'd rather you'd answer a little question."

He shook his head impatiently. "You have to understand the preliminaries, the steps by which this thing came into existence."

"Tell me about the thing that came into existence, and we'll talk about the steps later."

"No. I can't do that. I must go about it in my own way, Mr. Mason. I insist."

Once more Mason looked at his watch.

Dr. Macon said, "I will be brief. The modern physician, in order to serve his patients, must know something of their emotional natures, something of their backgrounds, something of the problems which confront them —the emotional crises, the—"

"I know all that," Mason said. "Tell me about Mrs. Hardisty."

"As soon as she came to me I realized there was some deep-seated worry, some lack of mental harmony. I suspected her domestic relations."

"And asked questions?"

"Not at once. I first went about getting her confidence."

"Then what?"

"Then I questioned her."

"What did you find out?"

"That, Mr. Mason, is confidential. I can't betray facts learned from a patient in making a diagnosis."

"Then why mention them?"

"Because I want you to realize that my knowledge of Milicent Hardisty is much more complete than yours could possibly be."

Mason settled down comfortably in a chair, lit a cigarette. "Because you investigated her mental condition in connection with your diagnosis?"

"Yes."

"Don't kid yourself," Mason said. "A lawyer does just as much probing into minds as a doctor does. What's more, a lawyer is better equipped and better trained to do it. You probably won't admit that. It doesn't make any difference whether you do or whether you don't, particularly since I haven't as yet had an opportunity to talk with Milicent Hardisty.

"Now you want to stall around for time, lay a foundation for impressing me, and put yourself in the position where you can tell me what you want to tell me, and hold out what you don't want me to know. If you think you can get away with it, go right ahead. It's going to take a little more time, but when we get done we'll understand each other that much better. You go right on with your prepared speech, and when you get finished, *I'll* do a little probing."

95

Dr. Macon smiled. "I'm afraid, Counselor, that you underestimate the facilities at the command of a trained physician. I know Milicent Hardisty much better than you could ever hope to know her by what you lawyers call cross-examination."

Mason gave himself to the enjoyment of his cigarette, made no comment.

Dr. Macon's professional bearing gradually reasserted itself. With the manner of a physician telling the patient just what the patient should know for his own good, and withholding everything that was not necessary for the patient to understand, Mr. Macon said, "Milicent Hardisty became a patient of mine. She had implicit trust in me. She confided in me. I came to know her innermost secrets. I was able to do her some good. I can tell you this much without betraying any confidence. She had devoted too much attention to her career, to the serious things in life. That over-emphasis on work left her with a secret hunger to be the center of attraction with some particular person —not a platonic attraction, but a sex attraction. For that reason she didn't question, even in her own mind, the motives of Jack Hardisty when he began rushing her off her feet in a whirlwind, impetuous courtship. Even if she *had* questioned his motives, I doubt if a realization of his duplicity would have stopped her. She was too thrilled with the novelty of having some man woo her, making of his courting not an intellectual pastime but a violent emotional activity.

"Jack Hardisty was shrewd enough to realize all that. Milicent has a good mind. She had in the past tried to appeal to persons upon an intellectual plane. Jack Hardisty decided the way to impress her was to sweep her off her feet, to bring ardor and passion to his wooing. It succeeded admirably."

Mason dropped ashes from the end of his cigarette into Dr. Macon's ash tray, said nothing.

96

"I'll tell you this—that after Vincent Blane established Jack Hardisty in business, Hardisty repaid his benefactor by embezzling money." Dr. Macon paused, dramatically.

Mason merely nodded.

Dr. Macon was obviously disappointed that his information came as no surprise. He frowned for a moment, then said, "Oh yes, the father retained you. Naturally, he told you about that."

"Go on," Mason said.

Dr. Macon thought for a minute, then began talking again, this time with more swift certainty. "I knew that Mrs. Hardisty was approaching a very definite crisis in her life. I knew that she had been unhappy for a long time. She had kept on, merely to preserve a semblance of happiness, and because she hesitated to make public confession that Jack Hardisty's interest in her had been financial. I think you will appreciate the feeling."

Mason made no comment.

"Late yesterday afternoon, when she failed to appear at my office to keep an appointment for a treatment, I took steps to ascertain that she was all right. As a result of those steps, I found that her husband had gone to Kenvale, and from there up to a mountain cabin owned by Mr. Blane. I learned that Mrs. Hardisty had followed him. I feared that, under some emotional unbalance, Mrs. Hardisty might suffer a nervous shock which would permanently impair her nervous and emotional stability."

"What did you do?" Mason asked.

"I started out to find Mrs. Hardisty."

"What time?"

"I would prefer to tell this in my own way, Mr. Mason. Your questions can come later. I believe you mentioned you wanted to probe my mind," and Dr. Macon's smile was icy.

"Go right ahead," Mason said, "pardon me. Simply because time is short I thought I could expedite matters.

97

But if you want to rehearse your story as you make it up, so as to be certain it's bomb-proof, go right ahead."

Dr. Macon said, "I am *not* making up this story. Whatever slight hesitancy you may notice is because I don't know exactly how much I can safely tell you without betraying confidential communications, and—"

"Never mind all that," Mason interrupted. "Go on with the story. What happened?"

"I drove toward the cabin in search of Mrs. Hardisty, that's all."

"Find her?"

"Yes."

"Go on," Mason said. "Tell it your way."

"I didn't find Mrs. Hardisty *at the cabin*. I found her in Kenvale. She was, I believe, following her unmarried sister, who was driving in a car ahead."

Dr. Macon paused for an appreciable interval. His face showed satisfaction; his eyes were triumphant. "I believe that about covers it. . . . I found Mrs. Hardisty in a serious nervous and emotional state. I kept her with me until approximately ten o'clock in the evening, until her nerves had responded to treatment. Then I drove her back to Kenvale, administered a hypodermic just before she entered the house, and told her to go to bed at once and to sleep late."

"That all of it?" Mason asked.

"That's enough, isn't it? I know that she was with me until after ten o'clock. I personally administered a hypodermic and know that immediately after taking that she would go to sleep and remain asleep for almost twelve hours."

"Finished?" Mason asked.

"Yes, sir. I have finished."

"All right," Mason said. "Now we'll start probing."

"Go right ahead."

"I believe you said you decided to go up to the cabin

in order to rescue Milicent from an experience which would disorganize her nerves and emotions."

"Substantially that. As usual with laymen, you have garbled the medical exactitude of expression; but we'll let it stand."

"And you found Milicent at Kenvale?"

"Yes."

"What time?"

"Well . . . let me see. . . . I should say that it was about —a man doesn't consult his watch under such circumstances, you know, even though attorneys are very fond of asking for exact time."

"Approximately what time?"

"Oh, it was sometime after six—perhaps around half past six."

"As late as seven?"

"I don't think so, yet it might have been."

"And not before six o'clock."

"No."

"And when you left your office, looking for Milicent, you knew that she was up at the cabin?"

"Yes."

"You mentioned that certain sources of information advised you on that point?"

"Well, yes. I secured that information."

"How?"

"I can't make any statement as to that."

"Why?"

"It would be betraying a confidence."

"Whose?"

"That's beside the point."

"A patient's?"

Dr. Macon thought over the question. A little gleam flashed in his eye, then disappeared. "Yes. The information came from a patient."

"And you realized that because Mrs. Hardisty was up

at the cabin and because Jack Hardisty was up there, there was a certain element of danger involved."

"What do you mean by danger? You must be more explicit, Counselor. You may mean danger to my patient's health, or physical danger, or—"

"That it was dangerous to the health of your patient to be up at the cabin."

"Yes."

"Then," Mason said with a smile, "how did it happen that immediately after you found her in Kenvale, in place of getting her as far away from the cabin as you could, you transported her right back up to that cabin?"

Dr. Macon's lips tightened. "I didn't say that."

"*I'm* saying it."

"I don't think that's a fair inference from what I said."

"It's not only a fair inference from what you said, but it's definitely indicated by your tire marks. Your automobile was up at that cabin."

"You haven't identified my tire marks. You haven't even seen my machine."

Mason said wearily, "Quit stalling. Did you or did you not take your car up to that cabin? Did you or did you not take Milicent up to that cabin after you found her in Kenvale?"

"I don't have to answer that question."

"You don't have to answer any of my questions," Mason said. "But those questions are going to be asked you by the police."

"There's a good chance the police may not even come to me."

"About one chance in a million."

"I don't agree with you."

"It doesn't make any difference whether you agree with me or not. You're going to be called on to answer that question. You're dead right in saying I have no authority

100

to make you answer it. Does that mean you're afraid to answer it here and now?"

"I simply refuse to answer that question."

"Why? Because the answer might incriminate you?"

"I give you no reason. I just don't have to answer that question, and I refuse to, that's all."

"No argument about that. Naturally, when you become afraid to answer questions, I am free to draw my own conclusions."

Dr. Macon stroked his chin nervously. "I took Milicent up there for certain reasons—connected with her health. It was a part of the treatment I had worked out for her. And I think you will agree with me, Counselor, that the minute I say *that,* no authority on earth can make me divulge what that treatment was or why I knew it was indicated."

"I don't think your medical exemption is that broad," Mason said, "but we'll let the answer stand for the minute. It is, of course, predicated upon the fact that you are her physician and that you are making that statement in that capacity."

"Certainly."

"How long have you been in love with her?" Mason asked.

Dr. Macon winced perceptibly, then said, as he made an attempt to regain his composure, "I suppose there is no limit to the insinuating, insulting questions—"

"You *are* in love with her, aren't you?"

"That is neither here nor there."

Mason said patiently, "It's very pertinent, Doctor. You tell a story which gets you into a position where you have to rely on your professional immunity to keep from answering interrogations. In other words, you have to show that *what* you did was done as a physician.

"Now, as the character of the physician merges into

that of the lover, the immunity of the physician vanishes."

"That is a matter we will leave with the police," Dr. Macon said with dignity.

"All right," Mason went on, "we'll get back to your story and my probing. You state that you gave Mrs. Hardisty a hypodermic which would put her to sleep."

"Yes."

"How soon would it take effect?"

"Within a very few minutes."

"Ten minutes?"

"An effect would be noticeable within that time, yes."

"She'd be asleep within half an hour?"

"Definitely."

"She couldn't have pretended to go to bed and then got up, taken a good strong cup of coffee or a caffein capsule and—"

"Definitely not," Dr. Macon interrupted.

"And you gave her that hypodermic just before she entered her house?"

"Yes."

"Acting as her physician?"

"Yes, of course."

"Not as her lover?"

"Mr. Mason, I'll thank you to—"

Mason silenced him with an upraised hand.

"You don't have to answer the question if you don't want to, Doctor. Just don't get steamed up about it."

"It's an insulting question, and I refuse to answer it on that ground—and on that ground alone."

"All right. You gave that hypodermic while she was sitting in the automobile and before she entered the house."

"Yes."

"How long have you been practicing, Doctor?"

"Something over twenty years."

"And during that time, have you *ever* given any other patient a hypodermic under similar circumstances?"

"What do you mean?"

"If you were acting as her physician, and solely in that capacity, you would naturally have gone into the house with the patient. You would have ordered her to prepare herself for bed. After she had got in bed, you would have administered a hypodermic. Then you would have waited a few minutes to make certain the hypodermic had taken effect, and then left the house, leaving instructions with whoever was in the house as to the care of the patient."

Dr. Macon's eyes avoided those of the lawyer.

"This business of sitting out in front of a house giving a woman a hypodermic, telling her to go in and put herself to bed, and then driving off, smacks of something furtive, something secretive, something that is highly irregular."

"Under the circumstances, I thought it was best to administer the hypodermic in that way. I reached that decision as a physician because of her symptoms, and I refuse to be questioned on that point."

"There was no reason why you weren't welcome in Mr. Blane's house?"

"Well . . . I don't think Mr. Blane approved of me as a physician for his daughter."

"Why?"

"I'm sure I couldn't tell you."

"It wasn't because he had some doubt as to your professional qualifications?"

"Certainly not."

"Then it must have been because of the personal relationship which was being built up."

"I prefer not to go into that."

"I can see that you might. . . . Well, there you are, Doctor. There are enough holes in your story right now to start you sweating, and I can think up a dozen more angles of attack."

"Then you don't believe my story?"

"It's incredible. It's unconvincing. It's contradictory. You can't make it stand up. You can't explain why you took her to the cabin, or why you gave her that hypodermic out in the car."

"I don't have to."

"Not to me, perhaps, but if you're telling a story to protect Milicent, it's something that *has* to stand up."

"What makes you think I am telling this to protect Milicent?"

"Because it's a fair inference that you met Milicent; that you went back up to the cabin with her because you knew Hardisty was up there; that you and she wanted to submit some proposition to Hardisty; that Hardisty was killed with a bullet from Milicent's gun, fired either by you or by Milicent; that you then extracted the bullet from Hardisty's body so it couldn't be traced to Milicent's gun."

"Absurd!"

"Well, we'll try another angle, then. Milicent Hardisty went up to the cabin. She met her husband up there. They had an argument. She accused him of a lot of things and insisted that he turn over to her the money and negotiable securities he had taken from the bank. He refused. She threatened him with the gun. There was a struggle for the possession of the gun. Jack Hardisty got shot, but death was not instantaneous. Milicent, in a frenzy, started running down the road from the cabin, hardly knowing what she was doing. Her sister, Adele, met her on the road. Milicent, in a panic, concealed her gun somewhere, or threw it away. Adele saw where this was. . . . Jack Hardisty was badly wounded. Milicent and Adele put him to bed. They then telephoned a frantic appeal to you. You dashed up to the cabin, examined Har-

104

disty and found that he was dead. He had died between the time he was put to bed and the time of your arrival. You then, swayed by your love for Milicent, proceeded to try to fix things up so that the murder was hopelessly obscured. You ran Hardisty's car over the grade. You removed the fatal bullet with your surgical instruments and took care to see that *it* would never be found. Adele may or may not have been in on the whole business. She probably was. You intended to deny any knowledge of what had happened, or that you had any connection with it. But the fact that I traced you through those automobile tires gave you a terrific jolt. . . . Now then, Doctor, let's hear what you have to say to that."

Dr. Macon shifted his position, said nothing.

At that moment, knuckles tapped gently on the door. The woman who had let Mason in opened the door and said apologetically, "I beg your pardon for disturbing you, Doctor, but a Mr. Jameson and Mr. McNair want to ask you some questions."

Mason said to Mr. Macon, "There it is. Jameson's the resident deputy at Kenvale, and Thomas L. McNair is a deputy from the district attorney's office. So you see, Doctor, you didn't have as much time as you thought you had. . . . Now let me tell you something. If Milicent Hardisty fired the bullet that killed her husband, either accidentally or in self-defense, or because he was just a rat who needed killing, now's the time for you to say so, and I'll see that she gets a fair break. But if you're trying to cover it up; if you think you can match wits with the law and come out on top, you're going to wind up by getting her convicted of first-degree murder. . . . Speak up."

Dr. Macon said, "I am not afraid of the law, Mr. Mason."

The lawyer studied him. "That's the worst of you doctors. Your training makes you too self-reliant. Just because you can advise patients on diet, you think you know how to advise 'em on everything. A lawyer wouldn't think he could snip out an appendix. But you're taking it on yourself to think out Milicent's defense to a charge of murder —and I think it's a lousy defense."

Dr. Macon said, with calm, professional dignity, "I have nothing to add to the story I have told you, Mr. Mason, and nothing to retract from it. Show the gentlemen in, Mable."

"Just a minute," Mason said. *"Just* a minute! Come in here, Mable, and close that door."

She hesitated a moment, then obeyed.

Mason said, "If those two find me here, they'll crucify you. The mere fact that I'm talking with you will make them think Milicent or Adele sent me to you. Is there any other way out?"

"Not out of this room. Where are they waiting, Mable?"

"In the hallway—and I don't think they'll wait long."

Mason said, "Tell them the doctor is busy with an emergency patient; that he'll see them just as soon as he completes the dressings." Then he turned to Dr. Macon. "Bandage up my head, Doctor. Leave one eye so I can see and that's all. Put my arm in a sling, spill on some disinfectants, and time things so they'll pass me in the corridor on the way in."

Dr. Macon nodded to the housekeeper, said to Mason, "Loosen your necktie and open your shirt."

The physician's hands moved with swift, deft skill. He wound bandage around Mason's head, placed his left arm in a sling, ripped wide adhesive tape into narrow ribbons, anchored the bandage with strips of tape, and sprinkled on antiseptic.

"All ready?" he asked Mason.

Mason's voice, coming from beneath the bandage, sounded strangely muffled. "Okay, Doctor. I'm warning

106

you for the last time—don't try to cover up. You can't get away with it."

Dr. Macon was crisply confident. "I can handle this situation very nicely," he said. "One of the things you fail to take into consideration, Counselor, is that a doctor is trained to keep his wits in an emergency."

Before Mason could reply, Dr. Macon threw open the door of the little den, said in a loud voice, "Show the gentlemen in, Mable."

Mason, his hat in his hand, walked out of the office, stooping slightly so as to disguise his figure.

Jameson and McNair passed him on the way in, keeping well over to one side so as not to brush against Mason's arm. Apparently they gave him no second glance.

Behind him, Mason heard Dr. Macon say, "Good evening, gentlemen, what can I do for you?"

The housekeeper held the outer door open for Mason.

"Good night," the lawyer muttered.

The woman made no answer, indignantly slammed the door as soon as Mason reached the porch.

12

◼

Paul Drake was waiting for Mason in the lobby of the Kenvale Hotel. "We've located Adele Blane, Perry."

"Where?"

"San Venito Hotel, Los Angeles. . . . That is, she *was* there. We've located her, and lost her again."

"How come?"

"The locating was easy," Drake said, "just a matter of leg work. We covered all the garages here. Didn't find anything. Didn't expect to. We checked all the garages at

Roxbury and found her car stored in the Acme Garage. The Acme Garage is near the bus depot. We checked on the time the car had been stored, and then started checking on the buses that left within an hour of that time. We found that a woman who answered Adele's description had gone to Los Angeles, traveling without baggage. I put operatives on the job, covering all the hotels near the Los Angeles bus terminal. We had a good description, and acted on the assumption that she'd been checking in without baggage. My operative finally located her at this little hotel. It's within about four blocks of the bus depot. She's registered under the name of Martha Stevens."

Mason knitted his brows. "That name's familiar, that's—"

"Housekeeper," Drake interposed.

"That's right. . . . Why would Adele Blane register under the name of her father's housekeeper?"

"Don't know," Drake said. "I can tell you one thing, Perry. . . . Martha Stevens isn't just any old housekeeper. She really rates, both with Vincent Blane and with the children. Incidentally, she gives Vincent Blane his hypodermics."

"What hypodermics?"

"Insulin."

"Is Blane diabetic?"

"Uh huh. Has to have an insulin shot twice a day. He can, of course, take them himself when he has to, but it's a lot more convenient to have someone else do the jabbing. . . . Martha does it."

"She's a nurse?"

"No. Milicent is, you know—or was. Milicent must have taught her how. . . . What did you find out just now, anything?"

Mason said, "Fat's being poured into the fire."

"How come?"

"The name on the paper Della handed me just before

108

I went out was that of Dr. Jefferson Macon, who lives at Roxbury."

Drake's eyes narrowed. "Milicent's physician?"

"Yes."

Drake snapped his fingers in exasperation. "*I* should have thought of that. What gave *you* the lead, Perry?"

"Tracks of new tires up at the cabin."

"Oh, *oh!*"

Mason said, "He's one of those calm, competent physicians and surgeons. He's been in love with Milicent for some time. Evidently knows pretty much about what's going on. . . . He got a tip that Hardisty was up at the cabin, and Milicent was going up, so he started out after Milicent, claims he met her on the outskirts of Kenvale. The evidence substantiates that part of it. What I'm afraid of is that he went *back* to the cabin with Milicent. The thing that bothers me most is that there must have been a note from Milicent to him, and there's just a chance that note may not have been destroyed."

"What gives you the idea of the note?" Drake asked.

"The time element. If Milicent had telephoned him that she was going to the cabin, Dr. Macon would have dropped everything and dashed up there after her, arriving a few minutes after she did. The way things look at this time, and from where I stand, Milicent must have written Dr. Macon a note. Someone delivered it—perhaps Martha Stevens. . . . Where's Della?"

"Upstairs."

Mason strode over to the room telephones, got Della Street on the line and said, "Just back, and going out. You haven't heard anything from Adele Blane?"

"No."

"Stick around. If she calls, have her keep under cover until I can get in touch with her. There's another angle to this thing. It doesn't look so good."

"See the doctor?"

"'Yes."

"Okay. I'll wait right here."

Mason hung up the telephone, walked back to Drake. "How did your man happen to lose her once he'd found her?" he asked.

"Adele?"

"Yes."

Drake said, "It's just one of those things, Perry. My man doesn't *think* that she was wise to him, but she *may* have been. She walked out of the hotel, evidently looking for a taxi, although there was nothing to tip off my operative that that was what she was doing. He tagged along fifty or seventy-five feet behind her. She was headed toward a taxi stand, as it turned out. Then, just as she was crossing a street, a taxi drew up, she flagged it, the signal changed, and they were gone. My man jumped on the running board of a private car, told the driver to follow the taxi. It just happened the driver didn't see things that way. He pulled over to the curb and started to argue. My man jumped off and tried to grab another cab and this motorist claimed it was a hold-up, and let out a squawk for the police. By the time the thing got straightened around, there was no chance of finding Adele Blane. . . . Those things happen in this business. . . . We're keeping the hotel covered, of course. She hasn't checked out. She'll be back."

Mason said, "That Martha Stevens business is the thing I can't understand. It worries me."

Drake said, "Want to go find this housekeeper and shake her down?"

Mason nodded. "My car's outside. Let's go, Paul."

110

13

■

Perry Mason slid his car to a gentle stop in front of the Blane residence.

"Looks dark," Drake said.

"The lights may be shielded," Mason observed, putting on the emergency brake. "Let's take a chance."

They walked up the echoing cement, pounded up the stairs to the porch. The sound of the doorbell was a sepulchral echo from the interior of the house.

Mason and Drake exchanged glances.

They rang twice more before giving up.

"Perhaps it's her night off," Drake said.

"Uh huh, we'll talk with Vincent Blane about her."

"Where are you going to find him?"

Mason said, "Ten to one there's a directors' meeting at that bank in Roxbury, and Blane is sitting there at the directors' table, very affably and suavely discussing ways and means and alibis."

"Want to bust in on him?" Drake asked.

"Why not?"

"Okay. Let's go."

While they were driving along at a thirty-five-mile-an-hour pace that seemed as awkward as the three-legged gait of a crippled greyhound, Drake said, "I can't get over Adele registering under the name of Martha Stevens. Why the devil didn't she think up a name?"

"Two reasons," Mason said.

"You're two ahead of me. I can't even think of one."

"One of them is that just in case anything ever came

111

up Adele might have fixed it up with Martha Stevens to swear that *she* was the one who occupied the room."

Drake said, "Well, it's an idea, but I don't get enthusiastic over it."

"The other one," Mason pointed out, "is that someone was going to meet Martha Stevens at the San Venito Hotel. Adele knew about the rendezvous, and decided to double for Martha Stevens. . . . Or else she's a stand-in to hold things in line until Martha can get there."

Drake shifted his position nervously. *"Now* you've got something, Perry. That last sounds more like it. I'll bet Martha Stevens is on her way to that hotel right now."

Mason said, "On a hunch, Paul, let's telephone your office from Roxbury. Send down a couple of operatives to check on the hotel, give them a description of Martha Stevens. Tell them to stick around and see what happens."

Drake said, "Step on it. It's going to take a little while to get men on the job. You can't pick up good operatives these days just by asking for them."

Entering the outskirts of Roxbury, Mason said, "While we're about it, we may as well drive by Hardisty's house. I want to see what the place looks like. . . . You know where it is?"

"I have the address," Drake said, pulling a memorandum book out of his pocket. "I haven't covered it personally. I've been busy on this other stuff."

"Okay. Let's hunt the place up. What's the address?"

"453 D Street."

Mason said, "Let's see how the streets run. Probably the letter streets are either north and south or east and west. . . . What street is this?"

Drake craned his neck out the car, said, "I can't tell. The sign is right next to the street light."

"There's a spotlight in the glove compartment. I'll slow down so you can take a look at the next one."

Drake gave vent to his feelings. "A detective's nightmare, these ornamental lamp posts with brackets for street names. You can't possible read these signs at night. You're looking at a black object silhouetted against a bright light. Cities have been buying those things for the last twenty-five years. What good does it do to advertise that it's a friendly city, thank you for your patronage and ask you to call again, when they're storing up ill will by sticking signs where strangers can't see 'em?"

"Why don't you go before a luncheon club and make a speech?"

"Some day I'm going to. It'll be *some* speech!"

"In the meantime take a look at this one," Mason observed slowing the car.

Drake tried to shield his eyes, said, "It's no use." He took the spotlight Mason pushed into his hand, directed the beam against the sign and said, "This is Jefferson Street."

"Okay. We'll turn to the right and see if we pick up the lettered streets."

The next street was A Street. Mason ran swiftly across B and C Streets to D, and turned left. Drake, with the aid of Mason's flashlight, began picking up numbers.

"This is the six-hundred block, two blocks more. About the middle of the block on the right-hand side. . . . Okay, Perry, take it easy now. . . . That looks like the place right ahead. There are lights in the windows."

Mason slowed the car to a scant fifteen miles an hour, crept past the lighted house, turned the corner to the right.

"Circling the block?" Drake asked.

"Yes. I want to take another look at it. What do you make of it, Paul?"

"Darned if I know. Lights are on and the shades are up. You can look right into the place, but there doesn't seem to be any sign of life."

Mason kept the car at the fifteen-mile-an-hour pace as he circled the block. "It *may* be a trap, Paul."

Drake said, "If no one's home, let's not go prowling around."

"On the other hand," Mason observed, "it *might* be that Adele Blane is in there. It's not apt to be Milicent Hardisty; it *can't* be Jack Hardisty. . . . Oh well, let's go see."

"Promise me you won't go in," Drake pleaded. "If no one's in there, and lights are on and perhaps the door unlocked, let's not stick our necks in a noose."

Mason said, "We'll see what it looks like."

They swung around the corner, back into D Street. Mason shifted into neutral and coasted up to the curb. He switched off the motor and lights and for a moment the two men sat in the car looking at the house.

"Front door's open a crack," Mason said. "You can see light around the edges."

"Uh huh."

"Of course, Paul, it may be that Vincent Blane has just stopped by. He may have a key."

"I tell you, Perry, it's a trap of some sort."

"Well, let's go up on the porch."

"Promise you won't go in?"

"Why all the holding back, Paul?"

"Because they'd accuse you of trying to find evidence and planning to conceal it. After all, Perry, we're playing this whole thing pretty much in the dark."

"I'll say we are," Mason agreed as they walked up the steps to the porch.

"Front door is open, all right," Mason said pressing a thumb against the bell button.

The jangling sound of the bell came from the interior of the house, but there was no other sign of life or motion.

114

Drake, looking through the front window, said suddenly, "Oh, Perry! Take a look here, will you?"

Mason moved over to his side. Through the open window could be seen a massive, antique, mahogany writing desk. A slanting door dropped down to form an apron for writing, back of it were a series of pigeonholes.

The splintered lock on the writing desk told its own story. Papers, strewn about the floor, had apparently been pulled out from the pigeonholes, hastily unfolded, read and discarded in a helter-skelter of confusion.

Drake said, "That settles it, Perry. Let's get out while the getting's good."

Mason hesitated a moment, standing in front of the window, then said with evident reluctance, "I guess that's the only sensible thing to do. If we notify the police, they'll always be suspicious we pulled the job, and then notified them after we had found and concealed what we wanted."

Drake turned and started eagerly for the stairs on the porch. Mason paused long enough to push against the front door.

"Don't do it, Perry," Drake pleaded.

Mason said, "Wait a minute, Paul. Something's wrong here. There's something behind the door. Something that yields just a little yet blocks the door—it's a man! I can see his feet!"

Drake, standing at the edge of the porch said, "All right, Perry, there's nothing we can do. Telephone the cops if you feel that way about it. We just won't give our names when we phone, that's all. Let them come and see what it's all about."

Mason hesitated for a moment, then squeezed through into the room.

Drake said with angry sarcasm, "Sure, go ahead! Stick your neck in! Leave a few fingerprints! You aren't in bad enough already. It won't hurt *you* to discover a couple more corpses, and when I try to renew *my* license another black mark more or less won't make any difference."

Mason said, "Perhaps there's something we can do, Paul," and peered around at the object behind the door.

The man who lay sprawled on the floor was somewhere in the late fifties. A spare individual with high cheek bones, a long, firm mouth, big-boned hands and long arms. His slow stertorous breathing was plainly audible once Mason had entered the room.

Mason said, "Oh, Paul, take a look. He's not dead, just knocked out. . . . Don't see any signs of a bullet wound —wait a minute, here's a gun."

Mason bent over the weapon. "A short-barreled .38," he said. "There's an odor of powder smoke. Looks as though it might have been fired. . . . But I still can't see any bullet wounds."

Drake said, "For the love of Mike, Perry, come on out of there. We'll telephone the police and let *them* wrestle with it."

Mason, completely absorbed with the problem of trying to deduce what happened, said, "This bird has a leather holster on his belt. Looks as though it was his gun. He may have been the one who did the shooting and then perhaps he got slugged. . . . Yes, here's a bruise up on the left temple, Paul. Looks as though it might have been done with a blackjack or—"

A siren sounded with that peculiarly throbbing sequence of low notes which comes before and after the high-pitched scream. A blood-red spotlight impaled Paul Drake on the porch, swept past him to throw a reddish light through the half-open front door.

Drake said with what was almost a groan, "I should have known it!"

A voice from the outside barked a gruff command. "Come out of that! Get your hands up!"

There were steps. Paul Drake's voice was raised in rapid explanations. Mason moved around the man's feet to appear at the half-open front door.

Two men, evidently local officers, carrying guns and five-celled flashlights, tried to hide nervousness behind a gruff exterior. "What's coming off here?" one of them demanded.

Mason said, "I'm Perry Mason, the lawyer. Milicent Hardisty is my client. I stopped by to see if she was home. We saw the lights and came up on the porch. As soon as I looked in the house, I saw something was wrong."

The second man said in a low voice, "It's Mason, all right. I've seen him before."

"How long have you been here?" the first officer asked.

"Just a matter of seconds," Mason said. "Just long enough to look inside. We were just starting to telephone for the police."

"Oh yeah? *This* guy was coming down off the porch when we spotted him with the light."

"Certainly."

"There's a telephone right here, ain't there?"

Mason said scornfully, "And if we'd used it, you'd have bawled us out for obscuring fingerprints."

"What's happened?" the officer asked.

Mason said, "I don't know. A man inside appears to have been slugged. There's a gun lying on the floor."

"Your gun?"

"Certainly not."

"You do any shooting?"

"Of course not."

"Hear any shot?"

"No. I'm not certain any were fired."

"Somebody telephoned headquarters," the officer said, "said that a shot had been fired in the Hardisty residence, and it looked like a murder."

"How long ago was this?" Mason asked.

"Seven or eight minutes."

Mason moved back through the half-opened door. "I don't see any evidences of a bullet wound," he said, "but there's a bruise on the left temple."

The two officers herded Drake in through the door, and then looked down at the unconscious figure.

"Shucks, that's George Crane," one of the men said.

"We'd better get him up off that floor," Mason said, "and see what can be done for him. Who's George Crane?"

"Merchant patrol, deputy constable. A good sort, does a little private work on the side."

Mason said, "We could lift him up on that couch."

"Okay. Let's do it. . . . Wait a minute; who's this man with you?"

"Paul Drake, head of the Drake Detective Agency."

"We'll take a look at his credentials first," the officer said.

Drake extracted a leather wallet from his pocket, passed it over. The men opened it, turned the cellophane-faced compartments, one at a time, looking at the cards. The leader said, "I guess you're okay," and handed the wallet back to Drake. They holstered their guns, snapped flashlights to their belts, then bent over the unconscious man on the floor. Mason and Drake helped them lift him to the couch. Almost immediately the eyelids fluttered, the tempo of the breathing changed, the muscles of the arm twitched.

Mason said, "Looks as though he's coming around. Find the bathroom, Paul; get towels soaked in cold water, and—"

"Just a minute," the officer in charge said. "You boys are staying right here with me, both of you. Frank, *you* get that wet towel."

The officer prowled around, found the bathroom. They

118

heard the sound of running water, then he was back with cold towels.

George Crane opened his eyes, stared groggily, then suddenly flung himself to a sitting position and started flailing about him with his arms.

The officers said, "Take it easy, George. Take it easy. You're okay."

Recognition came into the man's eyes.

"You're all right," the officer repeated soothingly.

"Where is she?" George Crane asked.

"Who?"

"The woman who slugged me."

"A woman?"

"Yes."

The officer looked questioningly at Mason, who shook his head.

The officer turned back to Crane. "There wasn't any woman, George, not when we got here. What happened?"

Crane raised a hand to his sore head, pulled down the wet towel, felt with exploring fingers along the line of the bruise on his temple, said, "The deputy sheriffs left me in charge until they could get a key to that writing desk, or a warrant to bust in, one or the other."

"Who has the key?" Mason asked.

"Mrs. Hardisty, I guess, but Mr. Blane said he thought her sister might also have a key. She has a key to the house."

"What happened?" the officer asked.

Crane pressed the towel back against his bruised head, said, "I left the place dark. Sort of thought someone might start prowling around and I could do a little good for myself by catching them red-handed. Nothing happened. I was sitting out here on the porch—and all of a sudden I knew someone was on the inside. I peeked through the window, cautious-like. I could see a woman

119

standing in front of that desk with a little flashlight playing on the stuff in the pigeonholes.

"The front door was locked. I figured she must have got in through the back door. If I tried to come in through the front, she'd put out the flashlight and make a run for it—so I sneaked around real quiet to the back. . . . Sure enough, the back door was open. I started pussyfooting through the house, heading for the front of the place. I must have tipped my hand. First thing I knew she was right in front of me. I had my gun in my right hand. I tried to grab her with my left, and she hit me on the right arm with a blackjack. I had the gun half raised when she cracked down. The jerk that came with the blow pulled the trigger on the gun—and that's all I remember."

"Did you hit her?"

"I don't know. . . . I don't think so. I wasn't aiming, just had the gun half up."

"Why didn't you use your flashlight?"

"I'm telling you I wanted to catch her red-handed. I thought she was still in the front room. I was pussyfooting through, not making no noise."

The officer said, "The trouble with you, George, is that you're half deaf. You *thought* you weren't making any noise, but—"

"Now that will do! I don't have to take any criticism from *you!*" George Crane interrupted angrily. *"You* ain't so smart. How about the time you were after the two burglars in the hardware store, and—"

The officer interrupted hastily, "Keep your shirt on, George. No one's criticizing you. We were just trying to find out how it happened. What time was this?"

"I don't know, rightly. Right around nine o'clock, I guess. What time is it now?"

"About fifteen or twenty minutes past nine."

"I guess it was right around nine, then."

"Someone telephoned in they heard a shot. Wouldn't leave a name. You don't know who that was, do you, George?"

Crane said irritably, "From the time I was halfway through the house, I don't know anything."

"You were over by the front door when we found you," Mason said. "Do you have any idea how you got there?"

Crane looked at him suspiciously. "Who are *you?*"

"We're the persons who found you," Mason said, smiling.

"Milicent Hardisty's lawyer," the officer explained.

Instant suspicion appeared in Crane's eyes. "What were *you* doing here?"

"We called to see if Mrs. Hardisty was home."

Crane started to say something, then apparently changed his mind, glanced significantly at the officers.

The officer in charge said, "I guess that's all. We know where we can get you two if we need you. . . . How about it, George, can you describe this woman?"

George Crane said pointedly, "Not while these guys are here."

The officer smiled. "I reckon he's right at that, boys."

Drake needed no second invitation. "Come on, Perry."

They walked out of the house, across the front porch, and down to where Mason had left his car parked. Drake said in an undertone, "Feel like running before they start shooting? It's an even-money bet they'll grab us before we get to the car."

Mason laughed, said, *"We're* okay, Paul. Something else is bothering me."

"What?"

"I'd just like to know if Adele Blane's car is still at the Acme Garage."

Drake said. "We can soon find out. That garage is just one block over from the main drag. My man says you can't miss it."

121

Mason, starting the motor, said, "I'm suspicious of the things you can't miss. . . . Wonder who it was that tclephoned in about that revolver shot."

"I don't know, and I don't suppose they're going to give *us* any information in case they do find out. . . . Swing to the left at the next corner, Perry, and then turn to the right."

Drake said, "Better let me go in, Perry. Two of us will make him suspicious. There's a way of handling these things."

Drake entered the garage, was gone for about five minutes, came back, jerked open the door of Mason's car, slid in beside the lawyer and slumped down on the seat.

"Well?" Mason asked.

Drake said, "Adele Blane took her car out exactly forty-five minutes ago."

Mason slammed the car into gear.

Drake, slumping dejectedly over against the corner of the seat, said, "One thing about a guy who works on your cases, Perry, he never needs to get bored. . . . Where are we going now?"

Mason, putting the car rapidly through the gears, said, "This time I'm going to *try* to get an interview before the police do."

"With Adele?" Drake asked.

"With Adele," Mason said, pushing the throttle down to the floorboard.

14

Utter silence surrounded the mountain cabin. The steady hissing of the gasoline lantern was the only sound that reached Harley Raymand's ears. There was no wind in the trees. The air was cold and still with that breathless chill which polishes stars into glittering brilliance.

It was, of course, absurd to think that the aura of death could make itself felt. Harley Raymand had seen death strike around him, to the right and to the left. He had trained himself to disregard danger. And yet, try as he would, a feeling persisted that gradually grew into a nervousness—a feeling that murder was in the air.

Those other deaths he had witnessed had been violent, full-blooded deaths in the heat of combat. Men, seeking to kill, had in turn, been killed. It was a fast game played in the open, and for high stakes—victory for the winner and death for the loser. But this was something different: a cold, sinister, silent death that struck furtively in the dark and then vanished, leaving behind only the body of its victim.

Harley realized that nine-tenths of his uneasiness was due to the feeling that he was being watched, that someone was keeping the cabin under a sinister surveillance.

He slipped out through the kitchen to the tree-shaded barbecue grounds, climbed the three long steps to the rustic porch, walked around to the front of the house, and stood by the porch rail, looking out at the stars.

Something flickered. A mere wisp of light that shone

like a fitful firefly in the trees, and then was gone. Harley waited, tense, watching. He saw the light again. This time it was stronger, sufficiently powerful so that he could see shadows cast on a pine tree. He knew then that someone was picking a surreptitious way through the forest, using a flashlight only at intervals.

Harley flattened himself in the shadows, and waited.

After some three minutes he saw two figures come out in the open. For a moment they were silhouetted against a beam of light flashed against the white granite outcropping. Then the flashlight was extinguished and all was darkness.

Harley thought he could hear the faint hiss of cautious whispers. Noiselessly he left the porch. Moving slowly, with the night stealth he had learned as part of his military training, he approached the rock.

The flashlight came on once more, shielded by cupped hands, throwing a spot of illumination on the ground at almost the exact spot where he had discovered the clock.

He was close enough to hear the whisper. "This is the place."

There was something vaguely familiar about that whisper. It was a woman's voice. Hands were scraping away at the ground. Harley caught a glimpse of those hands. Long, tapering fingers, slender, graceful hands and wrists—

"Adele!" he exclaimed.

The flashlight went out. There was a little scream, then a nervous, almost hysterical laugh, and Adele Blane said, "Harley! You scared ten years' growth right out of me. . . . Are you alone?"

"Yes. Who's with you?"

"Myrna Payson. . . . Harley, what happened to the clock?"

"I don't know. We couldn't find it. It isn't there."

"You searched for it?"

"Yes. . . . How did you get here? Why didn't you come to the cabin?"

"I went to Myrna's. We drove down to the first hairpin turn, left the car there and took a short cut. There's a trail over the ridge, only about half a mile of good walking. . . . I'm keeping myself out of circulation. . . . But if anyone offered me a hot drink, I could certainly use one."

"Got tea, coffee and chocolate," Harley said. "Why doesn't Myrna Payson say something?"

Myrna threw back her head and laughed. "What do you want me to say? As far as the hot drink is concerned, I'll say yes."

"Let's go up to the cabin," Adele suggested. "You'll have to keep the curtains drawn, Harley. I don't want anyone to know where I am."

"Why?"

"It's a long story. I can't tell you now. Harley, we've simply *got* to find where Jack hid that stuff he stole. It's around here somewhere. That's why he came up here with that spade. . . . And I keep thinking the clock has something to do with it."

"Well, let's go to the cabin and talk it over. There's no use looking at night."

"I suppose not. I thought that clock would be here, and I could tell something from that. I'd been telling Myrna about it. She felt it was the best clue of all."

"That's one of the first things they looked for."

"You told them about it?"

"Yes."

"And they didn't find it?"

"Not only that, but they can't find any evidence that anything was *ever* buried there."

"I wasn't sure you were still here," Adele said. "That's

125

why I was being so furtive. There's no one else in the cabin, Harley?"

"No."

"No one must know I'm here. Understand? Not a solitary soul."

"It's okay by me."

They entered the lighted cabin. Myrna Payson frankly sized up Harley, grinned, and said, "Hello, neighbor. You remember me? I'm the cowgirl who has the ranch over on the plateau. The cattlemen all think I'm going broke because I'm a 'fool woman'; and when I go to town, women look askance at me because I'm living 'all by myself, cooking for three cowboys.' On the one hand, I'm a fool; and on the other, a fallen woman. Pay your money and take your choice."

"And a darned loyal friend," Adele interposed.

Myrna Payson settled herself in a chair, thrust out high-heeled riding boots, fished a cloth sack of cigarette tobacco from her shirt pocket, and started rolling a cigarette, "Adele won't admit it, but I think she's wanted by the police, and concealing her will make me a real, sure-enough criminal."

Adele said, "Don't joke about it, Myrna. It's serious."

"I'm not joking," Myrna said, spilling rattling grains of tobacco into the brown paper.

"I have some cigarettes here," Harley said, reaching for the package of cigarettes.

Myrna said, "Drop one of those tailor-mades, and it will start a fire, but I never saw a fire started with a rolled cigarette. What's more, you can carry enough tobacco in a sack to really last you. . . . Well, we seem to have lost the clock. What's next, Adele?"

"I don't know," Adele admitted.

"Did you just drive up?" Harley asked Adele.

"I left my car in Roxbury. I got it out of the garage an

hour or so ago, and drove up to Myrna's ranch. She was out. I sat around twiddling my thumbs, waiting for her to come back."

"Went to town after provisions," Myrna explained. "Got back about half an hour ago and found Adele camped on my doorstep. She wanted to have reinforcements while she looked for the clock."

Adele laughed nervously and said, "Not only reinforcements, but a witness. Otherwise someone might think I'd planted the clock myself."

Myrna said practically, "You could have done it ten times over while I was in town."

"Myrna! *What* are you talking about?"

Myrna scraped a match on the sole of her shoe. "Don't lay your ears back, dear. I was just talking the way the police would."

"I don't like the police," Adele said.

"Don't blame you," Myrna said through a cloud of smoke. "I don't like them myself. Not as an institution. They're too nosey. I—"

She broke off abruptly as the sound of an automobile horn came to their ears. A moment later they heard the throbbing of a motor.

Adele said, "I *musn't* be found here, Harley."

"Why?"

"I can't tell you. I just *can't* be questioned right now. I'm keeping out of sight. You and Myrna are going to be the only ones who know. If anyone comes here they mustn't find me."

"How about Mrs. Payson?" Harley asked.

"We can't both hide very well," Adele said, "and—yet it wouldn't look right for her to be here with you. . . . What time is it, Harley?"

"Around ten thirty."

"Good Heavens!" Adele said.

Myrna Payson drew in a deep drag of smoke, exhaled slowly. Her words came lazily through the cigarette smoke, "It's all right, Adele. I haven't any reputation left, anyway. Go on and duck. Here they come."

They heard steps on the porch. Rodney Beaton's voice called, "Hello, the cabin! Are you still up?"

Adele slipped silently through the hallway into the bedroom.

Harley said reassuringly to Myrna Payson, "I won't have to invite him in——"

"Nonsense," she said. "I've come over for a visit. We're just talking, that's all. Invite him in as far as I'm concerned."

Harley went to the front door, threw it open, said, "Come on in, Beaton, and——"

He broke off as he saw that Rodney Beaton was not alone. Lola Strague was with him. Harley regained his verbal composure, said affably, "Why hello, Miss Strague. Come on in. Mrs. Payson and I were getting acquainted. I've been away so long that I hardly know the country any more."

Myrna Payson said easily, "Hello, Lola. Hello, Rod. I've been trying to get Harley to tell me about the war. He won't talk."

Harley noticed the tension between the two women, saw Lola Strague barricade herself behind a wall of watchful hostility. Myrna Payson, on the other hand, seemed thoroughly at ease, completely relaxed, but nevertheless gave the impression of being on her guard. Rodney Beaton was embarrassed, but Harley couldn't tell whether it was because he had found Myrna Payson visiting the cabin at such an hour, or because he didn't care to have Myrna know he had been out with Lola Strague.

"Is . . . anything wrong?" Harley asked somewhat awkwardly.

Rodney Beaton recovered his self-possession, laughed, "Heavens no! I forgot you don't realize my nocturnal habits. We've been out tending cameras."

"Any luck?" Harley asked.

Lola Strague accepted the chair Harley held for her, but sat stiffly erect. Beaton sprawled comfortably and informally. Myrna Payson continued to sit with her legs, incased in whipcords, extended in front of her. She was lounging easily in the chair, thoroughly enjoying herself so far as appearances were concerned.

Beaton said, "I've got three negatives to develop."

"Know what animals you've got?" Harley asked.

"No, I don't. I used to look for tracks, but now I've found it's a lot more fun just to develop the negatives."

"You have more than one camera?"

"Oh yes. I've got half a dozen scattered around."

"Don't you frighten the game away when you make the rounds?"

"No more," Beaton said. "I have a new system now. I go around and set the cameras after it gets dark. Then I climb up on a point where I have good observation, settle down, and wait. When one of those flashbulbs goes off it makes quite a flare, illuminates quite a bit of territory. I can tell, of course, what camera it is. I make a note of the location of the camera and the time the flashbulb was discharged. After I've waited two or three hours, I go around and pick out the plates, reset the cameras, go to my cabin, and develop them."

"And leave the cameras set?"

"Yes, I leave them until morning."

"I don't see why you watch them in the evening then."

"So I can pick up the first batch of plates and reload the cameras that have been set off before midnight. . . . Usually the best time is about four o'clock in the morning, but on the other hand I've had some very nice pictures around ten or eleven o'clock. . . . We were driving by on our way home and thought we'd drop in just to see—well, to see if you wanted anything, or—well, if you were all right."

Myrna Payson said with her slow drawl, "I reckon we all felt the same way. It would give me the creeps staying alone in a cabin where a murder had been committed. Harley says it doesn't bother him any."

Harley realized that his visitor had twice referred to him by his first name, so he laughed and said, "After all, if I were afraid, I'd hardly admit it to Myrna."

Lola Strague said somewhat stiffly, "Well, I think we'd better be going. It's really rather late for visiting, you know. I—"

Steps pounded up on the porch. Knuckles beat impatiently against the front door.

Myrna Payson said, "Well, it looks to me as though you're going to have a convention. I thought we were all here."

Harley started for the door. Before he had taken two steps Burt Strague's impatient voice called out, "Hey, Raymand! Is my sister in there?"

"Oh, *oh*—he's got the shotgun," Myrna Payson said.

Harley flung open the door.

Burt Strague, his voice sharp with anger, said to his sister, "Oh, there you are."

"Why, Burt! What's the matter?"

"Matter! Where on earth have you been?"

"Why, out with Rodney."

Burt repeated after her scornfully, "Oh yes, *out with Rodney!*"

Rodney Beaton moved forward. "Any objections?" he asked.

Lola managed to get between her brother and Rodney Beaton. "Burt!" she said, "don't be like that! What on

130

earth *is* the matter with you? I left a note telling you where I was going."

"Think again. You mean you *intended* to leave a note, but forgot to do it."

"Why Burt! I left it on the mantel, in the usual place."

Burt said irritably, "It wasn't there when I got there. I've been worried to death about you. . . . I'm sorry, Rod, if I seem to be a little brusque, but I've been worried."

"Burt, I've told you a dozen times that you're not to worry about me," Lola Strague said tartly. "I'm able to take care of myself."

"Oh, yes. A murderer's hanging around the country and I'm not supposed to worry. . . . Well, skip it. I've certainly been combing these hills for you, prowling the trails, looking all over. Incidentally, Rod, I walked through one of your camera traps down there by the fallen log where you got the picture of the squirrel."

"Tonight?" Rodney Beaton asked.

"Uh huh. Set off the flashlight. You probably got a good picture of me. As worried and annoyed as I was, I couldn't help but laugh when that flashlight burst into illumination, thinking about how you'd feel when you made the rounds of your camera traps, got what you thought was a swell deer picture, started to develop it and saw me plodding along the trail."

Beaton looked at his notebook. "That flashbulb exploded at nine-five," he said. "Do you mean to say you've been wandering around all the time since then?"

"I've been all *over* these mountain trails, I tell you. I even went up to the old mining tunnel."

Lola Strague became indignant. "What did you think *I'd* be doing in that old mining tunnel?"

"I didn't know," he said. "I got to the point where I was just a little bit crazy. I couldn't find you anywhere. . . . Just as a point of curiosity, where *were* you?"

131

"Out on that point where Rodney painted the picture of the sunset," Lola said. "From there we can look down on the valley and tell whenever a flashlight goes off."

Rodney Beaton said, "It's my new system. Beats blundering around over the trails, and scaring the game to death."

"And you mean to say you were up there *all* the evening?" Burt Strague asked, suspicion once more apparent in his voice. Rodney Beaton flushed.

"And you didn't hear me whistle? Why, I walked past that trail whistling that whistle I always use to call Lola!"

"Sorry," Beaton said somewhat stiffly.

"We didn't hear you," Lola said, then added hastily, "but of course, we weren't particularly listening for you. We weren't expecting to hear a whistle."

Myrna Payson laughed, said as though closing the subject, "Oh well, the lost is found, so why worry about it?"

The strained silence of tension settled on the room. Quite apparently Burt Strague wanted to say something, yet was managing with difficulty to restrain himself for the moment. Rodney Beaton, while retaining his poise, yet maintained toward Burt Strague the attitude of an annoyed grown-up dealing with an impudent child.

"Well," Myrna said, laughing and trying to make her voice casual, "someone say something."

No one did.

It was apparent that when that silence was broken, friendships would also be broken. Lola Strague was perhaps the only one who had it in her power to ward off what was coming, and for some reason she seemed incapable of doing so at the moment.

It was against that background of a silence charged with static hostility that Adele Blane's scream, high-pitched with terror, caught everyone by surprise.

Rodney Beaton whirled. "Good Lord, Raymand! That came from the room where Hardisty was murdered."

Myrna Payson, without a word, got to her feet, started running toward the closed door which led to the bedroom. She had taken no more than three steps when the door burst open. Adele Blane, her hair streaming back from her head, her eyeballs glistening in the light of the gasoline lantern, her mouth stretched open to its fullest capacity, screamed into the corridor.

Behind her there was a glimpse of a shadowy figure; another figure darted across the field of illumination from the doorway. An arm lashed out in a blow. There was the sound of a brief struggle.

Myrna Payson caught Adele in her arms, said, "There, there, Honey. Take it easy."

So imbued was Adele with the idea of flight, that she struggled to free herself, still screaming.

"What is it, Adele?" Rodney Beaton asked.

Harley Raymand said nothing. He pushed past the others, ran down the corridor which led to the bedroom. After a quick glance at Adele, Rodney Beaton crowded into the corridor behind him. Burt Strague took a hesitant step, then paused and turned to his sister. "Look here, Lola, you—"

She turned her back on him, and by that gesture shut off the unfinished sentence.

Harley Raymand went through the door of the bedroom, recoiled for a moment as the beam of a powerful flashlight stabbed him full in the face with blinding brilliance.

The voice of Jameson, the deputy sheriff, sounded crisp and competent. "It's all right, Raymand," he said. "We've just put Dr. Macon under arrest, and while we're here, we'll pick up Miss Adele Blane as a material witness."

Raymand fell back in sheer surprise. Jameson pushed his way into the corridor. Behind him an assistant deputy was wrestling the handcuffed, and still struggling Dr. Macon toward the doorway.

Jameson said to the chalk-faced Adele Blane, "And the next time, Miss Blane, you play the police for a bunch of suckers, you might remember that we're not *entirely* dumb."

<h1 style="text-align:center">15</h1>

In the midst of the excitement the arrival of Perry Mason and Paul Drake went unnoticed. Not even after Mason had pushed open the door of the cabin did anyone take immediate notice of him.

Dr. Macon had quit struggling against the grip of the handcuffs. Jameson, smilingly triumphant, was exhibiting the small black object which he held in the palm of his hand. "I'm calling on all of you," he said, "to witness that this is the bullet which Dr. Macon was trying to remove from the place where he had hidden it. I'm going to make a small scratch on the back of the bullet, so that we'll have a definite means of identification. . . . Do you care to make a statement, Doctor?"

Dr. Macon simply shook his head.

"And you, Miss Blane," Jameson said. "You, I believe, saw him enter through the window?"

She nodded.

"And do you care to make a statement at this time, telling what you saw, and explaining how you happened to be in that dark bedroom, apparently hiding from—"

Perry Mason stepped forward. "I don't think Miss Blane cares to make *any* statement at the present time," he said. "As you can plainly see, she's upset and frightened."

Jameson apparently saw Mason for the first time. "*You* again?"

Mason nodded and smiled.

"How the devil did you get here? We've had the place under surveillance."

Mason said, "Mr. Drake and I just arrived."

"Oh."

"And since I'm here, I'd like to talk with Miss Blane."

It was Jameson's turn to smile. "Unfortunately, Mr. Mason, we're taking Dr. Macon with us, and Miss Adele is going along as a material witness. Your arrival was opportune, but I'm afraid, Mr. Mason, it was just a little too late to save your client from sticking her head in a noose."

Jameson nodded to the deputy who was assisting him. "All right," he said, "let's get them out of here. And," he added after a moment during which he sized up the possibilities of the situation, "let's get them out of here fast."

It was as Dr. Macon and Adele were being hustled through the door, that Mason said to Paul Drake in an undertone, "Notice the reddish clay mud on Rodney Beaton's shoes."

Adele Blane flashed Mason an appealing look.

Mason surreptitiously lowered his right eye, raised an extended forefinger to his lips.

Jameson said to Rodney Beaton, "You have a car here, Beaton. Our car is parked down at the foot of the grade. Take us down there, will you please?"

Beaton said laughingly, "I suppose that's a request which is a command."

"We *could* commandeer your car," Jameson agreed, smiling. "We thought perhaps you'd prefer to do the driving."

"Come on," Beaton said.

Jameson lost no time in hustling his prisoners out of the house, taking care to give them no opportunity to talk with Perry Mason. The lawyer, holding himself completely aloof, stood over by the stone fireplace, leaning against the mantelpiece, smoking a cigarette.

At the very last moment Lola Strague said, "I'm going along with you, if you don't mind, Rod."

Beaton turned questioningly to Jameson.

"She was with you when you drove up?" the deputy asked.

"Yes," Beaton said.

"Okay. Bring her along."

Burt Strague started to say something, then checked himself, watched the others out through the front door, across the rustic porch, down the steps, and into the car.

After they had gone Myrna Payson said, "Well, despite our isolation, we manage to have a little excitement now and then."

"I presume Adele Blane came with you?" Mason asked.

She said, "That's your privilege, Mr. Mason."

"What is?"

"To presume anything you like."

Mason turned to glance questioningly at Harley Raymand.

"Really, Mr. Mason, I'd rather not," Raymand said.

"Okay," Mason announced.

Burt Strague said abruptly, "I don't like it. I don't like the way they're dragging Sis into this thing."

"Into what thing?" Mason asked.

"They've been out setting Rodney Beaton's cameras," Burt Strague said, *"but* they've been somewhere else."

"I noticed," Mason observed, "there were bits of a reddish clay soil on Rodney Beaton's shoes."

"Well, what of it?" Burt Strague asked suspiciously.

"I was just wondering where he might have picked up that reddish clay."

Burt Strague remained sullenly silent.

Mason went on after a moment, "There were traces of a similar clay on the bottoms of the trousers Jack

Hardisty was wearing when his body was found here in the cabin."

"You mean that clay might be a clue?" Burt Strague asked.

"It *might* be," Mason said.

"Oh well, that's different. I wasn't going to say anything if your inquiry was just idle curiosity, or an attempt to involve my sister, but I can tell you where Rod must have got that clay mud."

"Where?"

"Up at the mouth of the mining tunnel, back here in the mountains about half or three-quarters of a mile."

"That mud is *in* the tunnel?" Mason asked.

"No. It's on the trail about fifty or a hundred yards in front of the mining tunnel. It's where some of the dirt from the dump is softened up by drainage water that seeps out of the tunnel. The upper trail goes directly through it."

"I thought you said you were up there tonight," Raymand said.

"I was. I went by the lower trail. There are two trails up to the mining tunnel. I think originally there were old mining shacks on these cabin sites around here, and the men cut roads up to the mine. Those roads have gradually disintegrated until now there are only trails left."

"The upper trail goes from here to the tunnel?" Mason asked.

"Yes."

"And the lower trail?"

"That's more from the other side, over back of where Rodney Beaton has his cabin. . . . I went up there tonight, looking for my sister. Beaton's got cameras scattered around over all those trails. I touched off one of his flashguns tonight."

Mason said, "I think I should like to see that tunnel and go over the trails. Could we do it tonight?"

Strague hesitated. "I don't think Rodney would like it," he said. "He has his cameras set to pick up some game pictures. He hates to have the game disturbed at night. . . . However, if it's important—"

Mason said, "It's important. But under the circumstances, we'll wait and ask Beaton how he feels about it when he returns."

Myrna Payson said, "Oh bosh. Let's not put off any investigations simply on account of some pictures—unless, of course, you want to talk with Mr. Beaton."

Mason smiled. "I think we'll put it off until Mr. Beaton returns. Here he comes now."

In the moment of silence which followed, they could hear the sound of Rodney Beaton's automobile coming back up the grade to the cabin, and a moment later, Beaton and Lola Strague rejoined the little group.

"They played that pretty slick," Beaton said. "Had their car concealed down there, and kept the cabin under surveillance. They evidently knew when you and Adele came in, Myrna, but they didn't want to close the trap just then. They were waiting for additional game to walk in. I think they had an idea Dr. Macon might show up and try to tamper with some of the evidence. . . . Anyone know what actually happened in there?"

No one said anything.

"I gathered," Beaton said, "that Adele came with you, Myrna; that when she heard us coming she hid in that back room. It was dark in there, and when Dr. Macon showed up, he slipped in through the window and tried to remove the evidence he'd left there. . . . I presume that's the so-called fatal bullet they caught him taking away."

Lola Strague said, "Poor Adele. I don't blame her for being frightened to death."

Myrna Payson said nothing.

138

Mason said, "A matter came up while you were out, Beaton, that I think might well be discussed."

"What?"

"A certain reddish clay soil on your shoes."

Beaton looked at his shoes, said, "Yes. That's from up by the tunnel."

"I thought you said you weren't up there," Burt Strague said sharply.

Beaton regarded him for a moment with unwinking scrutiny, then said, "Not *in* the tunnel, youngster. As you probably know, that's on the upper trail about a hundred yards from the mouth of the tunnel. We went past there to cut down to the other trail to change the films in that camera. Incidentally, that's the one you tripped off when you walked through the trap."

"Then why didn't you meet me coming up the trail?" Burt Strague asked.

"Because we waited a while after the flash before we went down to the camera," Lola Strague said sharply.

"And I *do* wish, Burt, you'd either snap out of it or go home! After all, I'm free, white and twenty-one. I certainly don't need you to chaperone me, and I see no reason for airing these little grievances in front of—"

Mason said smoothly, "Well, as far as we're concerned, that's entirely outside the question. What we're interested in is a patch of red clay that was on Jack Hardisty's trousers when the body was found. Also there's some indication that a deliberate attempt was made to remove all traces of that mud from his shoes. I had asked Harley Raymand to look around here and see if he could find a place where the trail was muddy. I felt that it must have been near a creek bed or a spring, because it hadn't rained for a while, and—"

Beaton interrupted. "You should have asked me, Mr. Mason. Raymand isn't entirely familiar with the back country. I could have told you in a minute. There's only

139

one place anywhere around here where there's that type of mud; that's on the upper trail to the tunnel."

"Do you suppose," Mason asked, "we could take a look at it?"

"Sure. . . . But what would Jack Hardisty have been doing up there?"

As Mason made no answer, the significance of the situation apparently dawned on Rodney Beaton, and he gave a low whistle. "So *that's* it. Anybody been in that tunnel recently?"

They exchanged glances and head shakes.

"There's just a chance," Beaton said, "we might find something there."

Drake asked, "How about flashlights? Do we have plenty? I only have one, and—"

"I carry extra batteries and an extra bulb for mine," Beaton said. "Being out in the mountains at night as much as I am, I can't afford to take chances. . . . How about it, are we all going?"

Harley Raymand was the only one who hesitated; then, as he reached for the knob on the gasoline lantern, he smiled and said dryly, "It looks as though we're all going."

16

The little group strung out along the mountain trail. Flashlights, sending forth beams of light, looked like some weird procession of fireflies twisting a tortuous way through the night.

Rodney Beaton in the lead said, "Here's the place, Mr. Mason."

Mason inspected the muddy stretch in the trail.

Beaton went on to state, "This peculiar red clay came from the inside of the tunnel. It was brought out here and dumped when the tunnel was being excavated. There's a seepage of water that trickles down from the mouth of the tunnel. It keeps this patch of clay moist."

"Can you tell anything about these tracks?" Mason asked.

"Not much. You can see my tracks and Miss Strague's. Here are some deer tracks, and here's where a coyote has crossed over, but there are a lot of older tracks in the trail. Tracks made prior to the time Miss Strague and I came over it."

"Let's take a look inside the tunnel," Mason suggested.

They climbed a sharp incline to the mouth of the old tunnel.

"Know how deep this goes?" Mason asked.

"Only a couple of hundred feet," Beaton said. "They drifted in along a vein, and then lost their vein."

The inside of the tunnel was filled with musty, lifeless air. The smell of earth and rock had permeated the atmosphere.

"Gives me the creeps," Myrna Payson said. "I never could stand the inside of a tunnel. If it's all the same with you, I think I'll wait outside."

"I'll keep you company," Lola Strague said. "I feel somewhat the same about tunnels."

Burt Strague hesitated for a moment as though trying to find some excuse to stay with them, but Lola said sharply, "Go on in, Burt. Stay with the men."

Rodney Beaton, Burt Strague, Harley Raymand, Paul Drake and Perry Mason entered, walked to the far end of the tunnel. It was Rodney Beaton's flashlight that showed the significant excavation at the end.

141

"Looks as though someone had been getting ready to bury something here," Beaton said, indicating a shallow hole in the loose rock fragments which marked the end of the tunnel.

"Or," Mason said, "as though something had been buried and then dug up again."

Beaton became thoughtfully silent.

Drake glanced quickly at Perry Mason.

Mason swung his flashlight around the face of the tunnel. "Don't see any shovel here," he said.

All the flashlights explored the face of the tunnel.

"That's right," Burt Strague said, "there *isn't* any shovel."

"What's more," Mason pointed out, "this excavation wasn't made with an ordinary shovel. It was made with a garden spade with a six-and-a-half- or seven-and-a-half-inch blade. . . . You can see an imprint here of the whole blade."

Beaton bent forward. "Yes," he said, "and—"

Mason touched his shoulder. "I think," he announced, "we'll leave this bit of evidence just the way it is. Come on out—and let's try to keep from touching anything."

They walked silently out of the tunnel, explained the situation to Lola Strague and Myrna Payson.

Mason said, "I'd like to take a look at this lower trail that goes down by Beaton's cabin. . . . I take it that this mining tunnel is in Kern County."

"Oh yes," Beaton said. "It's well over the line."

"About how far?" Mason asked.

"Oh, I'd say a good half mile. Why? Would it make any difference?"

"It might," Mason conceded enigmatically.

Beaton said, "I'd better lead the way from here on. I reset the camera that caught the picture of Burt Strague on the trail. And if you don't mind, we'll circle around when we come to that point."

142.

Beaton went first down the trail, walking with long swinging strides, moving with an easy rhythm that covered ground rapidly.

After almost three hundred yards of walking down a good trail, Beaton slowed his pace, said, "The camera's right ahead. There it is."

His flashlight played on a camera set on a tripod, a synchronized flashbulb attached to one side of the shutter.

"How is that tripped?" Mason asked.

"I use a small silk thread stretched across the trail," Beaton said.

"And I blundered right through it," Burt Strague observed.

"Yes, here are your tracks," Raymand said, "—and you certainly were moving right along."

He indicated the tracks of Burt Strague's distinctive cowboy boots, tracks swinging along with the even regularity of a man hurrying along a mountain trail.

Burt Strague said impulsively, "I was worried about Sis. . . . I guess I acted a little foolish tonight, Rod. Forgive me, will you?"

Beaton's big hand shot out and clasped Burt Strague's. "Forget it. Your sister's rather a precious article, and I don't blame you for wanting to keep an eye on her."

17

◼

MURDER MAY HAVE ASTROLOGICAL BACKGROUND! DID STARS CONTROL DESTINY OF JACK HARDISTY?

**JURISDICTIONAL PROBLEM TEMPORARILY HALTS MURDER CASE.
AUTHORITIES OF KERN COUNTY INVESTIGATING NEW
EVIDENCE INDICATING MURDER MAY HAVE BEEN COMMITTED
IN ABANDONED MINING TUNNEL.**

Swiftly moving developments today characterized the Jack Hardisty murder case as one of the most baffling that has ever confronted local authorities.

Late yesterday afternoon, it was pointed out by the sheriff's office that the buried clock which Harley Raymand, an Army man invalided home, claims to have discovered near the scene of the murder, was set to what is known as sidereal, or star time.

Astronomers state that sidereal time is distinctly different from civil time, gaining a whole twenty-four hours during the course of a year. If, therefore, as now seems probable, the murderer of Jack Hardisty chose a moment for perpetrating his crime which would be under the most auspicious stellar influences, authorities feel they have a very definite clue.

The Bugle has commissioned one of the leading astrologers to cast the horoscope of Jack Hardisty. Jack Hardisty was born on July 3rd, which according to astrologists, makes him a *'Cancer,'* and astrologists point out that persons born under the sign of Cancer are divided into two classes—the active and the passive. They are thin-skinned, hypersensitive, and suffer deeply from wrongs, real or fancied. They are at times irrational in their emotions, and subject to ill health.

With recent developments indicating that the crime may have been committed either in Kern County, or so near the border of Los Angeles and Kern Counties that either county may have jurisdiction, the district attorney of Kern County is launching an independent investigation . . .

18

WATCHMAN SLUGGED IN HARDISTY HOME

FRAGMENT OF BROKEN SPECTACLE FIXES JURISDICTION IN MURDER CASE
MYSTERIOUS WOMAN SLUGS DEPUTY SHERIFF GUARDING HOME

Developments in the Hardisty murder case moved today with bewildering rapidity.

A person who is in close touch with the situation, but who wishes his name withheld, stated positively that Jack Hardisty had in his possession, at the time of his death, a large sum of money. There is a rumor that this money may have been removed from a Roxbury bank, where Hardisty had been employed up to the time of his death.

The sheriff's office, making a search of the Hardisty residence, was confronted with an antique locked desk. Because this was valuable as an antique Vincent P. Blane, the father-in-law of the victim, insisted that the lock should not be forced, but that officers should get a key either from Mrs. Hardisty or from Adele Blane. An attempt was made to secure a passkey, but because the antique writing desk had been recently fitted with a most modern lock, all efforts to open it in the usual routine manner proved futile.

Placing George Crane, a deputy constable and merchant patrol of Roxbury, in charge, police started trying to locate a key which would fit the lock. Mrs. Hardisty, who has steadfastly refused to make any statement concerning the case, finally consented to permit the authorities to use her key in opening the desk.

Shortly before nine o'clock, however, the telephone at police headquarters in Roxbury rang insistently. The voice of a man whom the police have not as yet been able to identify, advised them that he had heard the sound of a revolver shot at the Hardisty residence. Officers Frank Marigold and Jim Spencer, making a quick run to the scene, found George Crane unconscious from a blow with a blackjack administered a few minutes earlier by some unidentified woman at whom Crane had taken a shot, and whom he may have wounded. It was reported that Mrs. Hardisty's lawyer and private detective were also on the premises at the time. They were permitted to leave the premises without being searched. The writing desk had been forced open, and papers lay in a litter of confusion over the floor (see photograph on page three).

Coincident with this development, police have found evidence which definitely establishes the place where the crime was committed. Near a granite rock, some seventy-five yards from the Blane cabin where Hardisty's body was found, police found the broken fragment of a spectacle lens. A test by competent experts shows that was a fragment from Jack Hardisty's glasses—glasses which incidentally were not found on the body of the dead man.

In the face of this information, the district attorney of Kern County has stepped to one side, and jurisdiction will be held in Los Angeles County. . . .

19

Perry Mason threw the newspaper aside impatiently. Della Street's eyes met his. "You almost made it, Chief."

Mason said, "Almost doesn't count—not in this game."

"I notice that you were 'permitted to leave the premises without being searched.' "

Mason said bitterly, "Sure, that's a swell way of insinuating to the public that Paul Drake and I walked in and picked up ninety thousand bucks of stolen money, that we're going to use it as our fees. It's a nice little example of police innuendo."

"Can't you do something about that?"

Mason shook his head. "There's nothing libelous in the statement. We *were* permitted to leave the premises unsearched. That's the fact. I probably should have demanded that they search us, but we were so anxious to get out of there while the getting was good, that I didn't give the matter very much thought."

Della said, "Well, if the murderer did rely on astrology in order to pick an auspicious moment for committing the crime, he did a darn good job. This case certainly seems to be jinxed. First it's one thing and then it's another."

Mason lit a cigarette. "Trying a lawsuit is like changing a flat tire. Sometimes the jack works perfectly, the rim comes off, the new tire goes on, and you're on your way so smoothly that you hardly know you've had a flat. Sometimes everything goes wrong. The jack won't work, and when you finally get the car up, it rolls off the jack, the old tire sticks, the new rim won't go on. . . . And this is a case just like that, where everything has gone wrong to date."

"You've seen Mrs. Hardisty?"

"Yes."

"What does she say?"

"Nothing. Absolutely nothing."

"You mean she won't talk to you—as her attorney?"

"She won't say a word. Not only to the police, but to me."

"And how about Adele?"

"Adele Blane was hiding because she knew that her sister had written Dr. Macon a note that was what is known as indiscreet."

"Indiscreet in the Victorian or the legal sense?" Della Street asked with a smile.

"Both."

"And she's told that to the police?"

"I don't know what she's told the police. I doubt if even *she* does. They got her talking, and I understand

148

she made some contradictory statements. However, I doubt if they got *very* much out of her."

"Dr. Macon?"

"Dr. Macon is in love. He's one of those self-reliant surgeons who has been trained to tackle anything—and he *may* have killed Jack Hardisty."

"We're not representing him?" Della Street asked.

"Definitely not," Mason said. "We're representing Mrs. Jack Hardisty, and she's the *only* one we're representing. She's probably in love with Dr. Macon, knows some evidence that incriminates him, and therefore won't say a word, even to me.

"Another thing that bothers me is the cocksure attitude of the district attorney's office. I understand a new deputy is going to try it—a chap by the name of Thomas L. McNair. He's supposed to be a legal whirlwind. Came out here from the east somewhere, and has one of the most brilliant trial records of any young lawyer in the country. A percentage of nine convictions out of every ten cases tried—and for some reason or other, the district attorney's office is laughing up its sleeve, just lying in wait for me."

"And that's why you think this case is going to be one of those that will be like the flat tire that goes wrong."

Mason nodded moodily. "Something," he said, "is in the wind. There are certain angles of this case about which I know nothing. . . . You've always told me that it would be better for me to stay in my office and wait until cases came to me as other lawyers do, instead of getting out on the firing line. Well, this is once you can see how it works. From the start I've been one jump behind, and I *know* from the way they are acting, the district attorney's office is virtually certain of getting a conviction of both defendants."

"Who's representing Dr. Macon?" Della Street asked.

Mason grinned. "Dr. Macon. Trust the old self-reliant

surgeon for that. He's going to rush right in where angels fear to tread—"

The door opened somewhat explosively. Paul Drake, too excited even to bother with the formality of knocking, entered Mason's office. "They've got you, Perry!" he announced.

"Who has?"

"The D. A."

"On what?"

"That Hardisty case. They've got a dead open-and-shut case, a lead-pipe cinch. You'd better try to cop a plea."

"Has there been a confession?"

"No. But they've uncovered some evidence that makes it tighter than a drum. I don't know just what it is, but it has to do with a hypodermic syringe. I've found out that much. The district attorney let down the bars to one of the newspaper boys. He told this reporter that he just wanted to see your face when the evidence came in. He said in all the other cases you've tried, you've known in advance what the evidence was going to be, that this time, you're going to have the props knocked out from under you."

"Under those circumstances there's only one thing to do."

"What's that?"

Mason grinned. "Trust to cross-examination."

Drake said, "I think you'd better try to cop a plea, Perry. I don't think the district attorney will let you. He's been laying for you for a long time, and this time he thinks he has you where he wants you. But you *might* manage a plea."

Mason said, "I don't think I could get a plea. I wouldn't even try, unless Milicent Hardisty confessed to me that she was guilty and asked me to. . . . What have you found out about the sliver of spectacle lens, Paul?"

Drake's face showed a surprise. "Why," he said, "I thought the D. A.'s office had that all sewed up."

"What do you mean?"

"They've checked that piece of lens Harley Raymand gave them, and it matches up absolutely with Jack Hardisty's prescription."

"And how about the piece you have?"

"Why, it'll be the same of course."

"You mean you haven't had it tested?"

"No."

Mason said, "Have it tested."

"But, Perry, it'll be the same."

"How do you know it will?"

Drake thought the question over for a second or two, then grinned and said, "I'm just acting on the assumption that it will, I guess, Perry."

Mason nodded. "Have it checked, Paul."

20

The selection of the jury in the case of The People of the State of California *vs.* Milicent Blane and Jefferson Macon consumed a day and a half. At two o'clock in the afternoon of the second day, the jurors, having been sworn to try the case, settled back comfortably in their seats and looked expectantly at the district attorney.

Thomas L. McNair, the new, brilliant trial deputy, walked over to stand in front of the jurors to make his opening statement.

"Ladies and gentlemen of the jury, I will make no detailed statement of what we intend to prove. I shall let the evidence itself speak for the prosecution. I have long thought that it was presumptuous for a district attorney to tell intelligent men and women what the evidence means, or what he expects it to mean. I shall, therefore, merely content myself with showing that on the first day of October, of the present year, the defendants murdered Jack Hardisty, the husband of the defendant, Milicent Hardisty. I shall leave you, ladies and gentlemen, to deduce what happened. I will call as my first witness, Frank L. Wimblie, from the coroner's office."

Mr. Wimblie, having been duly sworn, testified to routine matters, the finding and identification of the body, the taking of photographs showing the position and condition of the body. He was followed on the stand by Dr. Claude Ritchie, one of the autopsy surgeons.

Dr. Ritchie, having duly qualified, testified that he had examined the body of Jack Hardisty; that death had been caused by hemorrhage and shock produced by a bullet wound which had been fired into the back of the decedent, entering just to the left side of the spine, ranging downward from behind the shoulder blade. The bullet had not been found in the body.

McNair sought to emphasize this point, so that the jury would be certain to get it. Despite the fact that he had, of course, known of this peculiar feature of the case for weeks, he managed to put surprise into his voice. "Did I understand you correctly, Doctor? The fatal bullet was *not* found in the body?"

"That is right. The bullet was not found."

"May I ask why?"

"It had been removed."

"It could not have dropped out?"

"Impossible."

"And it didn't go entirely through the body?"

"No, sir. There was no wound of exit."

McNair glanced significantly at the jury. "Now, Doctor, did you discover any other unusual condition in connection with your examination of that body?"

"I did."

"What was it?"

"A drug had been administered."

"Indeed! Can you tell us the nature of that drug?"

"In my opinion it was scopolamine."

"What is scopolamine, Doctor?"

"It is a drug which remains in the mother-liquors in the preparation of hyoscyamine and atropine from henbane seed, and those of Datura Stramonium."

"Of what use is scopolamine?"

"Among other things, scopolamine is used to detect, or rather to prevent, falsehoods."

"Can you explain that, Doctor?"

"Yes. Mixed with morphine, in proper proportions, scopolamine has the power of submerging certain inhibitory areas of the brain, yet at the same time leaving intact the patient's memory, hearing and powers of speech. In fact, the memory is sharpened beyond the normal conscious memory. Cases are on record in which persons under the influence of scopolamine have confessed to minor traffic crimes which had been completely forgotten during their ordinary everyday existence."

"And you state that this drug has a tendency to prevent lies?"

"That is right. Henry Morton Robinson cites, in *Science versus Crime,* experiments performed upon subjects under the influence of scopolamine in which they were urged to tell falsehoods and attempted to do so. They were incapable of falsifying their statements."

McNair glanced at the jury, then turned once more to the doctor. "What can you tell us, Doctor, about the *time* of death?"

153

"The time of death was between seven-thirty and ten o'clock in the evening of October first."

"Those represent extreme limits, Doctor?"

"Those represent extreme limits, yes, sir. If I were to express it according to the law of averages, I should say that the chances were about one in fifty that the man met his death between seven-thirty and seven-forty-five; that there was about one chance in fifty that he met his death between nine-forty-five and ten o'clock; I would say that there were about thirty chances out of fifty that the man met his death between eight-forty-five and nine o'clock in the evening."

"From the nature of the wound, was death instantaneous?"

"I would say not. I would say that the patient lived for perhaps five minutes to perhaps an hour. On an average, I would say probably a half hour. I am basing that answer upon the extent of the internal hemorrhage."

McNair turned to Perry Mason. "You may cross-examine."

Mason waited until the doctor's eyes turned to him, then asked, "Could you tell whether the decedent had been killed while he was in bed, or placed in bed after he had been shot?"

Dr. Ritchie said frankly, "I can't tell—that is, I cannot answer that question positively. You will understand that I am a physician and not a detective. I make certain *medical* deductions from the state of the body. That is all."

"I understand, Doctor. By the way, were there any powder burns upon the skin of the decedent?"

"No, sir."

"Did you examine the decedent's clothes?"

"Yes, sir."

"Did you notice whether there was any bullet hole in the coat the decedent had been wearing?"

"Yes, sir. There was such a hole."

154

"The coat, then, had evidently been removed *after* the shot was fired."

Dr. Ritchie smiled. "As I have stated, Counselor, I am not a detective. That inference is for the jury, not for me."

McNair's smile was almost a triumphant leer.

Mason nodded. "You are also a professional gambler, Doctor?"

Dr. Ritchie's smirk was lost in indignation. "Certainly not! That is an unwarranted question."

It was Mason's turn to smile. "Your making up of a list of chances, Doctor, indicated a knowledge not usually possessed by the physician. May I ask if your 'book' on the time of death based on the number of chances out of fifty is merely a casual estimate, or founded on mathematical calculations."

Dr. Ritchie hesitated while he mentally canvassed the possibilities of standing up to a cross-examination on the laws of probability. "An offhand estimate," he admitted sheepishly.

"And an estimate entirely outside the medical field?"

"Only in a manner of speaking."

"You have never had any experience in making book or determining the mathematical laws of chance?"

"Well . . . no."

"So you made an offhand estimate which is probably erroneous?"

"Well, it was a guess."

"So you were willing to make a guess, and swear to it as a fact?"

"Well, it was an estimate."

Mason bowed. "Thank you very much, Doctor. That is all."

Judge Canfield, somewhat by way of explanation, said to the jury, "Mr. Perry Mason is representing the defendant, Milicent Hardisty. Dr. Jefferson Macon is acting as his own counsel. I will, therefore, ask Dr. Macon if he has any questions on cross-examination."

"Yes," Dr. Macon said. "How did you determine the presence of scopolamine?"

"I relied principally upon the bromine test of Wormley, although I used both Gerrard's test and Wasicky's test."

"And it is your contention," Dr. Mason asked indignantly, "that I administered scopolamine to this person in order to make him talk and answer questions before he was murdered?"

Dr. Ritchie turned slightly toward the jury to deliver his answer. "That, Doctor," he said, "is your own suggestion. I am drawing no inferences. I am merely testifying to the facts that I found."

Dr. Macon muttered, "That's all."

"My next witness," McNair announced, "will necessarily be a hostile witness. I dislike to call him, but there is no alternative. I will call Vincent P. Blane, the father of the defendant, Milicent Hardisty."

Blane took the stand. His face showed plainly the effects of worry, but he was still very much master of himself, poised, courteous, dignified.

"Mr. Blane," McNair said, "because of your relationship to one of the defendants, it's going to be necessary for me to ask you leading questions."

Blane inclined his head in a courteous gesture of understanding.

"You knew that your son-in-law, Jack Hardisty, had embezzled money from the Roxbury Bank?"

"Yes, sir."

"There had been two embezzlements, I believe?"

"Yes, sir."

"One of ten thousand dollars?"

"That is the approximate amount."

"And when you refused to hush that up, Hardisty embezzled some ninety thousand dollars in cash, and ad-

156

vised you that if he was going to be short, he would make his embezzlement worth while; that if you kept him from going to jail and made good the ten thousand dollars he would return the ninety thousand dollars?"

"Not in exactly those words."

"But that was the gist of it?"

"The facts of the matter are, that before the bonding company would issue a bond on Mr. Hardisty, it required certain guarantees. The upshot of the matter was that I virtually agreed with the bonding company that if it would issue the bond, I would indemnify them against any loss."

"And did you ever recover the ninety thousand dollars?"

"No, sir."

"Or any part of it?"

"No, sir."

"That is all."

There was no cross-examination.

"I will now call another hostile witness," McNair said. "Adele Blane."

Adele Blane, plainly nervous, took the witness stand, was duly sworn, gave her name and address, and looked somewhat apprehensively at the vigorous young trial deputy who seemed to have that peculiar quality of focusing the attention of the entire courtroom upon himself.

"You are familiar with the location of the mountain cabin owned by your father, and in which the body of Jack Hardisty was found on October second, Miss Blane?"

"Yes, sir."

"And you were at the cabin on the afternoon of October first?"

"Yes, sir."

"Did you see Jack Hardisty there?"

"Yes, sir."

"What time?"

"I can't tell you the exact time. It was sometime after

157

four o'clock, and, I think, before four-forty-five, perhaps around four-twenty."

"And that is the best you can do so far as fixing the time is concerned?"

"Yes, sir."

"And you saw Jack Hardisty drive up?"

"Yes, sir."

"He stopped his car?"

"That's right."

"Did you see him take anything from his car?"

"Yes, sir."

"What?"

"A spade."

"Could you identify that spade if you saw it again?"

"No, sir."

"Were you alone at the time?"

"No, sir. A Mr. Raymand was with me."

"Mr. Harley Raymand?"

"That's right."

"And what did you do immediately after seeing Jack Hardisty at the cabin? Just describe your moves, please."

"Well, I drove back to Kenvale with Mr. Raymand. I took him to the Kenvale Hotel. I——"

"Just a minute," McNair interrupted. "Aren't you forgetting something? Didn't you see the defendant, Mrs. Hardisty, prior to that time?"

"Yes, that's right. I met her in an automobile."

"And where was she going?"

"I don't know."

"She was, however, driving on the road which led to the mountain cabin?"

"Well, yes."

"And you had some conversation with her?"

"Yes."

"You and Mr. Raymand?"

"Yes."

"And she asked if her husband was up at the cabin?"

"I believe so, yes."

"And you told her that her husband was up there?"

"Yes."

"And she promptly started her car and drove away in the direction of the cabin?"

"Well—well, yes."

"You know she went to the cabin, don't you, Miss Blane?"

"No, sir. I don't think she did go to the cabin."

"You left Mr. Raymand at the hotel, and turned around and speeded up the road to the cabin, didn't you?"

"Yes."

"Now, please tell us, Miss Blane, just what you found when you arrived at the cabin—or rather, just before you came to the road which turns off to the cabin."

"I found my sister."

"The defendant in this case?"

"Yes."

"What was she doing?"

"She was standing near an embankment."

"Did you notice any evidences of emotional upset—any external evidences?"

"She was crying. She was partially hysterical."

"Did she make any statement to you about a gun?"

Adele Blane looked around her, as though she were actually in a physical trap, instead of merely being on the witness stand under oath to tell the truth, and faced with the probing, searching questions of a vigorous prosecutor.

"Did she say anything about a gun?" McNair repeated.

"She said she had thrown her gun away."

"What were her exact words? Did she say she had thrown it down the canyon, on the brink of which she was standing?"

"No. She said she had thrown it— I can't remember."

"Did she say why?"

Adele looked appealingly at Perry Mason, but Mason sat silent. It was not the silence of defeat, but rather the silence of dignity. His eyes were steady. His face might have been carved from stone. His manner was confident. But, where the ordinary lawyer would have been throwing objections into the record, would have been storming and ranting, fighting for time, seeking to keep out damaging evidence, Mason was merely silent.

"Yes," Adele Blane said. "She told me why."

"What did she say?"

"She said that she was afraid."

"Afraid of what?"

"She didn't say."

"Afraid of herself?"

"She didn't say."

"Obviously," McNair said to the witness, "if she had been afraid of her husband, she would have kept the gun. Throwing it away means only that she was afraid of herself. Isn't that the way you understood her, Miss Blane?"

Mason came to his feet then, quietly, confidently. "Your Honor," he said, "I object to the question. It is argumentative. It is an attempt on the part of counsel to cross-examine his own witness. It calls for a conclusion of the witness. I have made no effort to prevent the *facts* from getting before the jury. Nor have I objected to the leading questions asked of this witness. But I do object to argumentative, improper questions such as these."

McNair started to argue, but Judge Canfield gestured him into silence. "The objection," he said, "is sustained. The question is clearly improper."

McNair pounced back on the witness, resuming his attack with a redoubled fury, convincing jurors and spectators, as well as the witness, that here was a man who could not be stopped, who was only stimulated by rebuffs to fight harder.

"What did your sister do after that?"

"She got in her car."

"Where was her car?"

"It was parked a short distance up the road."

"You mean by that it was parked on the main highway?"

"Yes."

"It was not parked on the side road which led up to your father's cabin."

"No."

"And then what did she do?"

"Followed me back to town."

"At your suggestion?"

"Yes."

"And then what happened?"

"When I got to Kenvale, I missed her."

"You mean that she deliberately avoided you?"

"I don't know. I only know that she didn't follow me to the house."

"And what did you do? Where did you go?"

"I went to Roxbury."

"Yes," McNair said, somewhat sneeringly, "you went to Roxbury. You went directly to the home of the defendant, Dr. Jefferson Macon. You asked for the doctor, and were advised he was out on a call. Isn't that right?"

"That is substantially correct."

"And you waited for Dr. Macon to return, did you not?"

"Yes."

"And when did he return?"

"At approximately ten-thirty."

"And what did you say to the defendant, Dr. Macon?"

"I asked him if he had seen my sister."

"And what did he say?"

161

"Just a moment," Judge Canfield said. "The jury will be instructed that at this particular time, any statement testified to by this witness as having been made by Dr. Macon will be received in evidence only as against the defendant, Macon, as a declaration made by him. It will not be binding upon the defendant, Hardisty, or be received as evidence against her. Proceed, Miss Blane, to answer the question."

She was close to tears now. "He said he had not seen my sister."

"Cross-examine," McNair snapped at Mason.

"No questions," Mason said with calm dignity.

Then McNair apparently went off on a detour. He began introducing evidence concerning the spade which belonged to Jack Hardisty. A witness testified that he had seen Hardisty using a spade in the garden. Was there anything peculiar about that spade, anything distinctive, McNair asked? And the witness stated that he had noticed the initials J. H. cut in the wood.

With something of a flourish, McNair sent an attendant scurrying to an anteroom. He returned with a spade which was duly presented to the witness for identification.

Yes, that was the spade. Those were the initials. He was satisfied that that was the identical spade he had seen in Jack Hardisty's hands.

There was no cross-examination.

McNair looked at the clock. It was approaching the hour of the afternoon adjournment. Obviously, McNair was looking for some peculiarly dramatic bit of evidence with which to close the first day's evidence.

"Charles Renfrew," he called.

Charles Renfrew proved to be a man in the early fifties, slow and deliberate of speech and motion, a man who quite evidently had no terror of cross-examination, but considered his sojourn on the witness stand with the

162

satisfaction of a man who enjoys being in the public eye.

He was, it seemed, a member of the police force of Roxbury. He had searched the grounds about the house where the defendant, Dr. Jefferson Macon, had his residence and his office.

McNair said, "Mr. Renfrew, I am going to show you a spade which has been marked for identification in this case, and ask you if you have seen that spade before."

"That's right," Renfrew said. "I found that spade—"

"The question was whether you had seen it before," McNair interrupted.

"Yes, sir. I have seen it before."

"When?"

"That day I made the search, October third."

"*Where* did you see it?"

"In a freshly spaded-up garden patch back of the garage on Dr. Macon's property."

"And you're certain this is the *same* spade you found at that place at that time?"

"Yes, sir."

McNair's smile was triumphant. "You don't, of course, know how this spade was transported from that mountain cabin to Dr. Macon's residence?"

Mason said, "Objected to, Your Honor, assuming a fact not in evidence as well as calling for a conclusion of the witness. There is no evidence that *this* was the spade Jack Hardisty had in his car."

McNair said instantly, "Counsel is right, Your Honor, I'll prove *that* tomorrow. In the meantime, I'll withdraw this question." He flashed a smile at the jurors.

Once more there was no cross-examination.

McNair went rapidly ahead. Rodney Beaton told of seeing the defendant, Milicent Hardisty, standing near the edge of a barranca by the roadway, some object in her hand, her arm drawn back. He couldn't swear, he

163

admitted, that she had actually thrown this object down the barranca. She might have changed her mind at the last minute. He also testified that the next day he and Lola Strague had been searching the vicinity of the granite outcropping. They had found a thirty-eight caliber revolver pressed down in the pine needles. He identified the gun.

Mason made no cross-examination.

Lola Strague, called as a witness, also told of finding the gun, and identified it. Then McNair, with a dramatic gesture, introduced in evidence records that showed this gun had been purchased by Vincent P. Blane two days before Christmas of 1941.

At that point McNair looked at the clock significantly and Judge Canfield, taking the hint, announced that it had reached the usual hour for the evening adjournment.

McNair left the courtroom wearing an expression of complete self-satisfaction wreathed all over his countenance. His exit was punctuated by brilliant flashes as news photographers took action shots for the morning editions.

21

McNair started his second day of taking testimony with a technique that left no doubt he was deliberately building this case upon a series of dramatic climaxes. Court attachés and jurors, who had become accustomed to the conventional dry-as-dust method of building a murder case from accusation to conviction, began to throng the courtroom, attracted by this dynamic personality, who was, for the moment, presenting so colorful a figure.

William L. Frankline was McNair's first witness of the day. Frankline, it seemed, was the deputy who had been with Jameson at the time Dr. Macon had been surprised at the Blane cabin, and Frankline testified in detail to steps they had taken to place the cabin under surveillance, and to seeing Adele Blane and Myrna Payson enter the cabin. Subsequently, Rodney Beaton and Lola Strague had arrived, and Adele had secreted herself in the dark bedroom where the body of Jack Hardisty had been found. Thereafter, Burt Strague had put in an appearance. Some minutes later, a skulking figure had been seen prowling around toward the back of the cabin. Having ascertained that the bedroom was dark, and apparently deserted, this figure had forced the window and entered the room. At that point the witness and one William N. Jameson, also a deputy sheriff, had approached the window, and at a signal simultaneously switched on flashlights, which had disclosed Adele Blane rushing screaming from the room, and the defendant, Dr. Macon, in the act of taking a bullet from its place of concealment behind a picture which hung on the wall of the bedroom. The bullet had been taken from Dr. Macon's hand as the handcuffs were put on him, and subsequently marked with a distinctive scratch for identification. And the witness unhesitatingly identified the bullet which McNair showed him as being that bullet.

"Cross-examine," McNair said to Perry Mason.

Mason regarded the witness thoughtfully. "You say that when you turned on your flashlights you saw this man in the act of removing a bullet from behind a picture?"

"Yes, sir."

Mason said, "In other words, you saw his hand behind the framed picture. When you jerked the hand out you found there was a bullet in it, and from that, you deduced that he was removing a bullet from behind the picture. Is that right?"

"Well—you might put it that way."

"And for all you know," Mason said, "the defendant, Macon, instead of taking something out, may have been—" Mason broke off abruptly as his eye caught the smirk on McNair's face. "I'll withdraw that question," he said calmly, "and there are no further questions of this witness."

McNair was suddenly furious. He started to get up, apparently to make some objection, then dropped back into his chair. He frowned thoughtfully.

Mason drew toward himself a pad of paper, scribbled a note. "McNair wanted me to force Frankline to admit that Macon might have been putting the bullet *in* instead of taking it *out*. Something fishy here. Hold your hat."

He walked over to hand the note to Della Street.

Judge Canfield looked at Dr. Macon. "Does the defendant, Macon, have any questions?"

"No questions."

"Any redirect, Mr. McNair?"

"No . . . no, Your Honor. That's all." McNair seemed definitely nonplussed, but a moment later he called Dr. Kelmont Pringle.

Dr. Pringle qualified himself as an expert criminologist, laboratory technician, a specialist in forensic medicine and toxicology, and an expert on ballistics.

"Handing you the bullet which has previously been identified and received in evidence," McNair said, "I will ask you if you examined that bullet and made certain tests with it."

"I did."

"I now hand you a thirty-eight caliber Colt revolver, which I am asking at this time may be marked for identification. I will ask you, Doctor, if you fired any test bullets through that gun."

"I did."

"And did you, with the aid of a comparison microscope, compare them with the bullet which I have just handed you?"

"I did."

"And were the bullets fired from this weapon of the same general description as the bullet which you hold in your hand, Doctor?"

"Yes, sir."

"Now then, Doctor, by the aid of the comparison microscope, did you determine whether or not this bullet which you hold in your hand had been fired *from this very weapon* to which I have directed your attention?"

"I did."

"Was that bullet so fired from this gun, Doctor?"

There was the trace of a frosty twinkle in Dr. Pringle's eyes. "It was not!"

Judge Canfield looked down at McNair's smiling countenance, glanced at Perry Mason, leaned forward on the bench, said, "I beg your pardon, Doctor. Did I understand the answer to be that the bullet was *not* fired from that weapon?"

"That is right," Dr. Pringle said. "The bullet definitely was not fired from this weapon."

Dr. Macon settled back in his seat with the relaxation which comes with relief from a great tension.

There was no expression whatever on the face of Milicent Hardisty.

Perry Mason kept his eyes fastened steadily on the witness.

"Now then," McNair went on, "since it appears that the bullet was *not* fired from this .38 revolver which I have handed you, Doctor, I will ask if you made any further examination of that bullet or found out anything further in connection with it?"

"Yes, sir. I did."

"I direct your attention, Doctor, to certain reddish-brown stains appearing on the bullet, and, at one particular place, to a certain bit of dried reddish material."

"Yes, sir."

"What is that material, Doctor?"

"It is animal tissue which has become dehydrated by exposure to the air."

"And these reddish-brown stains, Doctor, what are these?"

"Those are blood."

"Have you made tests with that tissue and with the blood?"

"Yes, sir."

"And have your tests definitely ascertained whether that is or is not blood?"

"Yes, sir. They have. It is blood."

"Now, Doctor, please listen carefully to this question. Assuming that, on the first day of October, nineteen hundred and forty-two, a man was killed by a bullet fired from a thirty-eight caliber revolver, is there anything about this bullet which would enable you, as an expert, to tell whether or not this particular bullet which you are now holding in your hand was the fatal bullet which brought about the death of this individual on October first, nineteen hundred and forty-two?"

"Yes," Dr. Pringle said. "There is something about this bullet which would enable me to answer that question."

"Will you please state to the jury just what that is, Doctor?"

"I tested the blood on that bullet both by the precipitin

168

test and by microscopic measurement with a micrometer eyepiece."

"And what did you find?"

"I found that the erythrocyte was one thirty-five hun-dredth of an inch in diameter."

"What is the erythrocyte, Doctor?"

"The red blood corpuscle."

McNair turned abruptly to Mason. "Do you have any cross-examination?"

Mason hesitated, then said, "Yes."

He regarded Dr. Pringle with a frown. "Doctor, that is a most peculiar way to give your testimony."

"I answered questions."

"You did, indeed. You volunteered no conclusions."

"No, sir. I was asked, at this time, only for facts."

"You stated that you convinced yourself the diameter of the red blood corpuscle was one thirty-five hundredth of an inch."

"Yes, sir."

Mason paused for a moment, then went ahead cau-tiously. "Doctor, I am not absolutely certain of my in-formation, but it seems to me that the red blood corpuscle of the human being is one thirty-two hundredth of an inch in diameter."

"That is right."

Mason shifted his position.

Judge Canfield leaned abruptly forward, resting his el-bows on his desk, looking down at the witness. "Doctor, I want to eliminate the possibility of a misunderstanding. Do I understand from your testimony that the red blood corpuscles of the blood on this bullet were one thirty-five hundredth of an inch in diameter?"

"Yes, sir."

"And that those of a human being are one thirty-two hundredth of an inch in diameter?"

"That is right."

"Then do I understand, Doctor, that the blood on this bullet was *not* human blood?"

"That is correct, Your Honor."

Judge Canfield looked at the district attorney with an expression of exasperation on his face, settled back in his cushioned chair and said to Mason, "Proceed with the cross-examination, Counselor."

"Then, since the blood on this bullet was not human blood," Mason said, "did you determine what blood it was?"

"Yes, sir. It was the blood of a dog. The erythrocyte of a dog measures one thirty-five hundredth of an inch, and, of all the domestic animals, its size is the nearest to that of the human. I satisfied myself by the precipitin test that the blood on this bullet was that of a dog."

"Then," Mason went on, feeling his way cautiously, "you would state, would you not, Doctor, that under no possible circumstances could this bullet have been the fatal bullet which brought about the death of Jack Hardisty?"

"Yes. This bullet has had no contact with human flesh. This bullet has been fired into a dog."

Mason said abruptly, "That is all."

McNair smiled and bowed at Mason. "Thank you, Counselor, for clarifying my case for me."

Judge Canfield, plainly irritated, started to make some comment, then checked himself. After all, Perry Mason could very well take care of himself.

"That's all for the present, Doctor," McNair said. "I'll call my next witness, Fred Hermann."

Fred Hermann came forward and took the witness stand. He, too, it seemed, was on the police force at Roxbury. He was of the stolid, phlegmatic type. Appearing as a witness in this case was, to him, merely another chore which interfered with his daily routine. He acted as

170

indifferent and bored as though he had been called to court to testify in connection with some routine misdemeanor arrest he had made the night before.

When he had given his name, age, residence and occupation, McNair asked him, "You are familiar with the witness, Renfrew, who was on the stand yesterday?"

"Yes, sir."

"Did you accompany him to the office and residence of the defendant, Dr. Jefferson Macon, on the third day of October of the present year?"

"Yes, sir."

"Were you with him when he discovered the spade?"

"Yes, sir."

"I will show you that spade which was introduced in evidence, Mr. Hermann, and ask you whether you have ever seen it before."

The witness took the spade, turned it over slowly, methodically, deliberately, in his big hands, handed it back to the prosecutor. "Yes, sir," he said, "that's the one."

"And where was it that this spade was found?"

"On the north side of the garage. There was a little garden patch there and some freshly dug earth."

"And what did you do with reference to that earth," McNair asked, glancing triumphantly at Perry Mason.

"We started digging."

"And how deep did you dig?"

"About three feet."

"And what did you find?"

Hermann turned so that he was looking at the jury. "We found," he announced, "the body of a big dog. There was a bullet hole in the body, but we couldn't find any bullet; that had been removed."

McNair was smiling now. "Your witness," he said to Mason.

"No questions," Mason announced.

Judge Canfield, looking at the clock, said, "It's time for the noon recess. Court will reconvene at two o'clock."

There was a swirl of activity on the part of spectators as Judge Canfield retired to his chambers. Newspaper reporters, rushing forward, took flashlight photographs of McNair, showing him smiling triumphantly. They had Dr. Pringle pose for them on the witness stand. They did not ask Perry Mason for photographs.

22

Perry Mason and Della Street sat in the curtained booth of a little restaurant around the corner from Mason's office, eating a luncheon which consisted mostly of tea and cigarettes.

"I don't get that about the dog," Della Street said.

Mason said, "The thing works out mathematically from the district attorney's point of view. Dr. Macon met Milicent as she was coming back from the cabin. She told him about the new embezzlement, about Jack Hardisty having ninety thousand dollars in cash that he was using as blackmail. Dr. Macon suggested that they return to the cabin, that he give Hardisty a hypodermic of scopolamine that would make him talk, and betray the hiding place of the stolen currency."

Della Street sipped her tea. "I understand that, all right," she said. "According to that theory they must have gone back and give him a hypodermic. After that he became violent and one of them shot him. But where does the dog come in?"

"Don't you see? Dr. Macon would know that they'd recover the fatal bullet, that they'd check it with Milicent's gun, that then they'd have a dead open-and-shut case. So he extracted the bullet and hid it."

"But how could he shoot it into a dog after—"

"He didn't. McNair's betting that Macon got another gun of the same caliber, killed a dog with it, removed the bullet, buried the dog, and intended to conceal the bullet in the cabin in such a place that it would be found sooner or later. When the authorities found it, they'd think they'd discovered the fatal bullet where it had been concealed by Dr. Macon. They'd test it and find, to their surprise, that it *didn't* fit Milicent Hardisty's gun."

"Then Dr. Macon was putting the bullet behind the picture, instead of taking it out, when he was apprehended?" Della Street asked.

"Exactly," Mason said, "and I almost led with my chin by asking on cross-examination if he might not have been putting something *in* instead of taking something *out*. . . . I caught myself just in time on that one."

"What gave you the tip-off?"

"Something in the way McNair was watching me, some expression on the witness' face. . . . But I walked right into that dog business. I had to. I was in a position where I either had to stop my cross-examination, which would have made it look as though I were afraid of the truth, or go ahead and bring out the point which crucified my client."

"Why didn't McNair bring it out under direct examination?"

"Because it hurts my case more when I bring it out on cross-examination. . . . Those are sharp tactics, and I'm going to get even with him."

"How?"

"I don't know *yet*," Mason admitted.

173

Della Street stirred the few grounds of tea in the bottom of the tea cup. "I could almost cry," she confessed. "—You can see what happened. If Milicent Hardisty didn't kill her husband, Dr. Macon at least thinks she did, and tried to protect her. In doing it, he dragged them both into the mess. . . . Or Dr. Macon killed him, and Mrs. Hardisty is trying to protect him. Either way we're licked—and McNair is so sneering, so soaked up with triumph, that he just makes me *sick*. I'd like to pull his hair out, a handful at a time. I'd like to—" Rage choked her words.

Mason smiled, "Don't get excited, Della. Use your head instead. . . . There's one discrepancy in the evidence that I doubt if McNair's thought of."

"What is it?"

Mason grinned at her. "Wait until he puts Jameson on the stand."

"I don't get it."

"I don't think anyone's thought of it," Mason said, "but I'm going to make them do a lot of thinking about it."

"But you can't possibly work out any theory that will get Milicent Hardisty acquitted—can you?"

"I don't know," Mason said somberly. "Perhaps not, but I can mix the case up so that a lot of that supercilious smirk will come off McNair's face and—"

Mason broke off as he heard Paul Drake's voice asking the proprietor, "Is Perry Mason eating in here today?"

Mason pulled back the curtain of the booth. "Hello, Paul, what have you got?"

Paul Drake entered the booth. His face wore a grin. Under his arm he carried a small package wrapped in newspaper and tied tightly with a string.

Della Street moved over so he could sit down beside her. Drake put the package on the table.

174

Almost instantly a faint but unmistakable sound of steady ticking became apparent.

"The buried clock?" Mason asked.

Drake nodded.

"Where did you get it?"

"Harley Raymand found it buried just under the surface of the ground, about ten feet from the edge of the rock where it had been concealed the first time."

"How far from where the broken spectacle lens was found?" Mason asked.

"Not very far. . . . Harley Raymand tied up the package and wrote his name across the wrapper. I wrote my name just above his, and tied it up in another wrapping. . . . Do you want to open it in court?"

Mason thought it over for a moment, then said, "We'll put Harley Raymand on the stand, and let him identify his signature. . . . We've got to do that before the clock runs down. It's a twenty-four-hour clock, isn't it, Paul?"

"Yes."

"And what time did the clock say—that is, was it slow or fast or—"

Drake said, "The darned clock is two hours and forty-five minutes fast."

Mason pulled a piece of paper from his pocket and did some rapid figuring. "That puts it almost exactly on sidereal time, Paul. As I get it, sidereal time would be about three hours and forty-five minutes fast today, but our time has been moved up an hour on account of the war. That means the clock is almost exactly on sidereal time."

Drake gave a low whistle. "Perhaps that tag about the stars wasn't just a pipedream, Perry. Why the devil should a man want a clock that keeps time with the stars —and why should it be buried around in different places?"

Mason's grin was gleeful. "That, my boy, is a question we'll try to dump in the lap of Thomas L. McNair."

"They won't let you put it in the case, Perry."

Mason said, "I know they won't, but they'll have a hard time keeping me from putting it in the minds of jurors."

23

As court reconvened at two o'clock, Thomas L. McNair sat at the table reserved for counsel for the prosecution, his face wearing a smile which just missed being a smirk.

Judge Canfield said, "The Jurors are all present, and the defendants are in court, gentlemen. Are you ready to proceed, Mr. McNair?"

"Just a moment, Your Honor," Mason said, getting to his feet. "At this time I wish to ask permission of the court to introduce some testimony out of order."

"Upon what ground is the motion made, Mr. Mason?"

"Upon the ground that the evidence is, in its nature, perishable. It will not keep until I have an opportunity to put it on in regular order."

"Why not?" McNair demanded truculently.

Mason turned to him with a little smile. "It's rather difficult to explain that without going into the nature of the evidence, Counselor."

McNair said sneeringly, "Go ahead and explain it. I'd like to know what evidence you have that is, as you so aptly term it, perishable."

Mason turned back to Judge Canfield. "It is a clock,

Your Honor. A clock which was found buried near the alleged scene of the crime. It—"

"And what does a clock have to do with it?" McNair interrupted sarcastically. "Good Heavens, Your Honor. Here we have a plain open-and-shut murder case, and counsel for the defendant comes into court with a clock which was buried near the scene of the crime. It's incompetent, it's irrelevant, it's immaterial. It can't possibly be introduced in evidence."

Mason said, "Of course, Your Honor, I will connect it up at the proper time; otherwise, the jurors can be instructed to disregard it."

"But what is perishable about a clock?" McNair demanded. "You've got the clock. I guess it will keep, won't it? I never heard of a clock spoiling. You might pickle it in alcohol."

There was a well-defined titter from the courtroom. A few smiles appeared on the faces of the jurors, and McNair grinned gleefully at these smiling faces.

Mason said, "The *clock* will keep, but the *time* shown on the dial of the clock won't. If the Court please, I am advised that this clock is now exactly two hours and forty-four and one-half minutes faster than our Pacific War Time. And inasmuch as our Pacific War Time is advanced one hour, that makes the clock exactly three hours, forty-four and one-half minutes ahead of our sun time."

Judge Canfield frowned. "And exactly what is the possible significance of that fact, Mr. Mason? In other words, why should that evidence be preserved?"

"Because," Mason said, "as of this date, sidereal time is exactly three hours, forty-four minutes, thirty-nine and one-half seconds in the advance of civil time. It is, therefore, plainly apparent that this ordinary alarm clock has been carefully adjusted so that it is keeping exact sidereal time, and inasmuch as I understand it is a twenty-four-hour clock, unless it is received in evidence, and the jury given an opportunity to note the time shown on the dial, the clock will have run down, and this valuable bit of evidence will have been destroyed."

"And what possible connection can the stars have with this murder?" McNair demanded.

Mason said, "That, Your Honor, is one of the things I will connect up when it comes time to put on my case. All I am asking at the present time is permission to identify this clock so that the testimony may be preserved while it is available."

Judge Canfield said, "I will grant your motion."

Harley Raymand, being duly sworn, testified that he had first found the buried clock on October first, the date of the murder. That at that time, the clock, according to his best recollection, was some twenty-five minutes slow. That he had again found it on October second. That he had thereafter made search for the clock and had failed to find it again until approximately eleven o'clock on the morning of the present day when he had happened to hear a ticking noise; that he had listened carefully, located the spot in the ground from which that ticking was heard, and had uncovered what appeared to him to be exactly the same clock, in exactly the same box. That at this time, however, the clock was some two hours and forty-five minutes fast, as compared with his own watch.

"What did you do with this clock?" Mason asked.

"I wrapped it up in a package, wrote my name across the wrapping at the suggestion of Mr. Paul Drake. I then delivered the package to Mr. Paul Drake who also wrote his name directly above mine."

Perry Mason asked, "Open this package, which I hand you, and see if it is the same package which you so gave to Mr. Drake."

The jurors were leaning forward in their seats.

178

"Your Honor," McNair said, "not only do I object to the introduction of this evidence at this time as being out of order, but I object to it as incompetent, irrelevant and immaterial."

Judge Canfield said, "The Court has already ruled on the motion permitting Mr. Mason to put on the evidence at this time, and out of order. The Court will reserve a ruling on the objection that it is incompetent, irrelevant and immaterial until the defendant presents his case. Or, to put the matter in another way, the Court will admit the evidence temporarily, subject to a motion on the part of the prosecution to strike it out in the event it is not properly connected up."

"That," Mason announced, "is all I ask, Your Honor."

Harley Raymand unwrapped the package, took out a small wooden box. He opened this box and disclosed an alarm clock ticking competently away.

Mason made some show of taking out his watch and comparing it with the dial of the clock, then he turned to consult the electric clock at the back of the courtroom. "May we call to the attention of the jury at this time, that the clock is apparently two hours, forty-four minutes and forty seconds fast."

Judge Canfield said, his voice showing the interest he was taking, "It will be so noted for the record."

McNair, plainly irritated that the smooth progress of his case had been interrupted, said, "Your Honor, I would like to reserve my cross-examination of this witness until after the Court has finally ruled whether the evidence is admissible."

"So ordered," Judge Canfield said. "Has any test of this clock been made for fingerprints, Mr. Mason?"

Mason said suavely, "Apparently not, Your Honor. I would like very much to have the Court instruct the fingerprint expert from the sheriff's office to make proper tests."

"That will be the order," Judge Canfield said. "Now, Mr. McNair, do you wish to proceed with your case?"

"Yes," McNair said truculently. "Now that we have disposed of the horoscopes and the astrology, we might get down to brass tacks. I will call Mr. William N. Jameson as my next witness."

Jameson, duly sworn, testified to finding the body of Hardisty in the cabin. Testified also to matters of technical routine, identifying maps, photographs, and presenting all the groundwork necessary in murder cases.

Gradually, however, having disposed of these details, McNair once more started building to a dramatic climax. "Did you," McNair asked, "on the second day of October of this year, have occasion to go to Roxbury with me?"

"Yes, sir."

"And where did you go when you arrived in Roxbury?"

"To the place where the defendant, Dr. Macon, has his office and residence."

"Did you see Dr. Macon at that time?"

"I did."

"Who else was present?"

"You and Dr. Macon, that's all."

"And, following that interview, did you have occasion to examine Dr. Macon's automobile?"

"I did."

"Who was present at that time?"

"No one. You were talking with Dr. Macon. I slipped out and went through his car."

"What did you find, if anything?"

"Dr. Macon's surgical bag was in the back of the automobile. I looked through it. In a little leather medicine case which held a lot of small bottles, I found a bottle

180

which seemed to be filled with cotton. I took out the cork and pulled out the cotton. Concealed in the cotton was a piece of paper."

McNair looked at the clock. "Any writing on this piece of paper?"

"Yes, sir."

"Would you recognize this piece of paper if you saw it again?"

"Yes, sir."

McNair said, with a smile, "I am offering the paper at this time for identification. Tomorrow, I will introduce handwriting experts to show that the writing on the paper is in the handwriting of the defendant, Milicent Hardisty. In the meantime, purely for the purposes of identification, I wish to read into the record the message which is upon this paper."

"No objection," Mason said, as Judge Canfield regarded him with a puzzled frown.

McNair read:

"Dearest Jeff:

Jack has done the most awful thing. I couldn't believe him capable of such perfidy, such dastardly treachery. He is up at the cabin. I am going up there for a show-down. If the worst comes to the worst, you won't see me again. Don't think too badly of me. I can't see why men like him are permitted to live. . . .

There is no use my trying to tell you how much you have meant to me, Jeff, or what you have done for me. No matter what happens, I will feel that I am always close to you and that you will be close to me.

I am hoping that I can get Jack to see the light, and right, at least in part, the great wrong he's done my father. For what he has done to me, I do not

181

care. I can stand that. It will be humiliating, but I can take it. But I can't take what he has done to Father, lying down. As this may be good-bye, I want you to know how very, very much you have meant to me. Your kind patience, your steady faith, your friendship, and the more which lay behind all this have been inspiration and sustenance to me. Good-bye, my dear.

Yours,
Milicent."

McNair handed the paper to the clerk of the court with a flourish. "Please mark this for identification," he said, "as the prosecution's exhibit."

McNair turned to Perry Mason, glancing triumphantly at the clock, to note that once more the papers would have an opportunity to record a dramatic finish to the afternoon session.

"Is that all of your direct examination of this witness?" Judge Canfield asked.

"Yes, Your Honor. It is approximately four forty-five, and—"

Judge Canfield ignored the hint. "Cross-examine," he said to Mason.

For a moment there was a flash of consternation on McNair's face. It was quite apparent he had hoped Judge Canfield would adjourn court, and there was a sympathetic glint in the eyes of His Honor as he glanced at Perry Mason.

Mason faced the witness.

"You worked up this case, Mr. Jameson?" he asked.

"What do you mean by that?"

"You endeavored to uncover evidence in it?"

"Yes."

"You did everything possible to unearth significant facts which might be considered as clues?"

"Yes."

"Did you look down in that canyon to see if you could find the weapon which the defendant, Milicent Hardisty, is said to have thrown down there?"

Jameson smiled. "That was hardly necessary."

"And why not?" Mason asked.

"Because her gun was found—where she had tried to hide it after the murder."

"I see," Mason said. "Therefore, it wasn't necessary to look for a gun she might have thrown down into the canyon."

"That's right."

"In other words, having found Mrs. Hardisty's gun, there was no use searching for any other."

"That's right."

"You knew Mrs. Hardisty told her sister she had tossed her gun over an embankment?"

"She *claimed* that," Jameson grinned.

"And as an officer looking up facts in the case, you checked that statement by looking in the place she had indicated?"

"No, by looking in the place she actually hid the murder gun."

"You don't *know* it was the murder gun?"

"Well . . . of course—it was the gun she must have used."

"And you are willing to swear there is no gun lying on the steep slope where Mrs. Hardisty told her sister she had thrown *a* gun?"

"I couldn't *swear* that, but I'd bet a million dollars on it."

Judge Canfield said sternly, "The witness will answer questions and refrain from extraneous comments."

Mason smiled. "You don't *know* this is the gun that killed Hardisty. You don't *know* Mrs. Hardisty put the gun where it was found, and, as an officer, you have never checked Mrs. Hardisty's story that she had thrown the gun which was in her purse down that steep slope. Is that right?"

"Well, I—do you mean, Mr. Mason, that the defendant had *two* guns?"

"*I* don't mean anything," Mason said. "I'm merely asking questions. I am trying to find out what investigation was made."

"Well, we didn't look in the bottom of the canyon, or along the slope."

"So, for all you *know*, Mrs. Hardisty *may* have thrown a gun in the bottom of the canyon."

"Well, yes."

"And that gun *may* have been the thirty-eight caliber revolver which fired the bullet which the witness Pringle states had been used to bring about the death of a dog."

"Well . . . I wouldn't say that."

"The question is argumentative," McNair objected.

"I think it's within the bounds of legitimate cross-examination, however; bearing in mind that counsel is entitled to show bias of the witness," Judge Canfield ruled, "the objection is overruled. Answer the question."

"Well . . . I—oh, I suppose she *could* have shot a dog and buried it at Dr. Macon's house, and then driven up to the top of the canyon and thrown the gun away," the witness said, with an attempt at sarcasm.

"And," Mason observed, "by the same token, she could have driven up a little farther, killed a dog near the cabin and thrown the gun away. Then Dr. Macon could have found the dog, carried it home and buried it near his garage, couldn't he?"

"Well, I don't think it happened that way."

"Oh, you don't *think* it happened that way?"

"No."

"So what you want this jury to do is to return a verdict

184

of guilty of murder in the first degree, predicated on the way you *think* the thing must have happened."

"Well, not exactly that."

"Pardon me. I must have misunderstood you. That was what I understood to be the effect of what you said, the position you had adopted."

"Well, there wasn't any dog up at the cabin."

"How do you know?"

"Well, there was no evidence that a dog had been up there."

"And just what would you expect to find in the line of evidence that would convince you a dog *had* been up there, Mr. Jameson. Speaking as a detective, what evidence would you say a dog might leave behind that would tell you he had been there?"

Jameson tried to think of some answer, and failed.

"Come, come," Mason said. "It's approaching the hour of adjournment. Can't you answer the question?"

"Well . . . well, no dog was up there."

"And how do you know?"

"Well, I just *know* he wasn't."

"What convinced you?"

"There's no evidence a *dog* had been up there."

"That," Mason announced, "brings us right back to the point where you stalled before. What evidence would you expect to have found?"

"Well, there weren't any footprints."

"Did you look for footprints?"

"Yes."

"For a dog's footprints?"

Jameson smiled. "Yes, sir."

"And that was before there had been any evidence connecting a dog with this case?"

"Well, I guess so, yes."

"But you were looking for a *dog's* footprints?"

"Well . . . well, not exactly."

185

"Then you *weren't* looking for a dog's footprints?"

"Well, not for a dog's. We were looking the ground over."

"And did you notice any dog's footprints?"

"No, sir."

"How about a coyote's prints? Is that what those tracks were?"

Jameson thought for a moment and said, "Well, now wait a minute. . . . Now, come to think of it, I'm not going to swear there *weren't* any dog's footprints, Mr. Mason."

"And you aren't going to swear that there *were* any?"

"Well, no."

"In other words, you didn't look for a dog's footprints?"

"Well, not particularly. Come to think of it, the footprints of a coyote are so much like—no sir, I'm not going to swear one way or another."

"You have already sworn both ways," Mason said. "First that no dog was up there, second that you looked specifically for a dog's footprints, third that you *didn't* look for a dog's footprints, fourth, that a dog *may* have been up there. . . . Now, what is the fact."

Jameson said irritably, "Oh, go ahead, twist everything I say around—"

"The witness will answer questions," Judge Canfield admonished.

"What," Mason asked suavely, "is the fact?"

"I don't know," Jameson said.

Mason smiled. "Thank you, Mr. Jameson, and *that* is all."

Judge Canfield glanced at the clock, then down at the discomfited McNair. "It appears," the judge said slowly and deliberately, "that it has *now* reached the time for the afternoon adjournment."

24

■

Perry Mason paced the floor of his office, head thrust forward, thumbs pushed into the armholes of his vest. Della Street, sitting over at her secretarial desk, watched him silently, her eyes filled with solicitude.

For nearly an hour now, Mason had been pacing rhythmically back and forth, occasionally pausing to light a cigarette or to fling himself into the big swivel chair behind his desk. Then after a few moments he'd restlessly push back the chair, and once more begin his pacing back and forth.

It was almost nine o'clock when he said abruptly, "Unless I can think of some way of tying in the astronomical angle of this case, I'm licked."

Della Street welcomed the opportunity to let words furnish a safety valve for his pent-up nervousness. "Can't you let the clock speak for itself? Surely it isn't just a coincidence that it's keeping perfect sidereal time."

"I could let the clock speak for itself," Mason said, "if I could get it introduced in evidence; but how the devil am I going to prove that it has anything whatever to do with the murder?"

"It was found near the scene of the murder."

"I know," Mason said, "I can stand up and argue till I'm black in the face. 'Here's a buried clock. It was found near the scene of the murder. First, the day of the murder, second, the day after the murder. Then it disappeared until weeks later when we're trying the case'— and Judge Canfield will look at me with that cold, analytical gaze of his, and say, 'And suppose all that is true, Mr. Mason. What possible connection does all that have with the case?' And what am I going to say to him then?"

"I don't know," Della admitted.

"Neither do I," Mason said.

"But there must be someone connected with the case that is interested in astrology."

Mason said, "I'm not so darned sure. That astrological angle was a good thing to use as a red herring to try and get the Kern County district attorney interested, but a person doesn't have to know sidereal time in order to play around with astrology. A person wants sidereal time for just one purpose: that is, to locate a star."

"Please explain again how you can locate a star by a clock," she said.

Mason said, "The heavens consist of a circle of three hundred and sixty degrees. The earth rotates through that circle every twenty-four hours. That means fifteen degrees to an hour. . . . All right, astronomers divide the heavens into degrees, minutes and seconds of arc, then translate those degrees, minutes and seconds of arc into hours, minutes and seconds of *time*. They give each star a so-called right ascension, which is in reality nothing but its distance east or west of a given point in the heavens, and a declination, which is nothing but its distance to the north or south of the celestial equator."

"I still don't see how that helps," Della Street said.

"An astronomer has a telescope on what is known as an equatorial mounting. The east and west motion is at right angles to the axis of the earth. As the telescope moves, an indicator moves along graduated circles. Once you know the right ascension and declination of a star, you only have to check that against the sidereal time of that particular locality, swing the telescope along the graduated circle, elevate it to the proper declination, and you're looking at the star in question. . . . Now, you tell me what on earth that has to do with the murder of Jack Hardisty."

"I can't," she said, and laughed.

"Neither can I," Mason said, "and unless I can find some way of doing it, I'm damned apt to have a client convicted of first-degree murder."

"Do you think she's guilty?"

Mason said, "It depends on what you mean by being guilty."

"Do you think she killed him?"

"She may have," Mason conceded. "But it wasn't cold-blooded, premeditated murder. It was an accident, something that came about as a result of some unforeseen development. . . . But she *may* have pulled the trigger."

"Then why doesn't she tell the complete circumstances?"

"She's afraid to, because in doing that she'll implicate someone else. . . . But what we're up against, Della, is a double-barreled crime."

"How do you mean?"

"How does this look? Jack Hardisty takes that money up to the tunnel. He buries it. Someone gives him a dose of scopolamine, he talks, and under the influence of the drug babbles his secret. That person goes up and gets the money; or else goes up and finds that some other person has been there first and got the money."

"And you don't think that was Milicent Hardisty?"

Mason shook his head. "If Milicent Hardisty or Doctor Macon had found that money, they'd have gone to Mr. Blane and said, 'Here you are. Here's the money.' That's what all the trouble was about. They were trying to get that money back because it was going to put Blane in a spot if he had to make it good."

"Yes. I can see that," Della Street admitted.

"Therefore," Mason said, "some third party intervened. Someone has the ninety thousand dollars, and is hanging onto it. And just as sure as you're a foot high, that clock is connected with it in some way, and simply because I can't find out what the connection is before court convenes tomorrow morning, I'm letting a damned whippersnapper, smart-Aleck deputy district attorney nail my hide up against the side of the tannery."

"It isn't as bad as that," she protested. "You've certainly got them worried about that gun now."

Mason nodded almost absently, said, "The gun is a red herring. It's a little salt in an open wound, but that clock—damn it, Della, that clock *means* something!"

"Can't we tie it in with something else?" she asked. "The piece of broken glass from the spectacle lens, for instance. Couldn't you—"

Paul Drake's knuckles pounded three knocks on the door, then after a pause, two short sharp knocks.

"Paul Drake," Mason said. "Let him in."

Della Street opened the door. Drake, grinning on the threshold said, "You've got them all churned up, Perry. They're up there prowling around that canyon with spotlights, flares, floodlights, flashlights, and matches. Jameson swears he's going to go into court tomorrow morning and prove to you that there isn't a gun anywhere in the whole damned barranca."

Mason nodded absently, said, "I thought he'd do that. I may have some fun with him on cross-examination, but that isn't telling me how the clock ties into the case."

"Astrology?" Drake suggested.

Mason said, "That astrological angle is interesting, but it's nothing we can sell Judge Canfield."

Drake said, "Don't be too certain. I've just found out something about Mrs. Payson."

"What about *her?*"

"She's a student of astrology."

Mason gave that matter frowning consideration.

"I'm going to tell you something else," Drake said.

190

"You'll remember that when we got the oculist's report on that sliver of broken spectacle lens, he said he thought it was from Jack Hardisty's spectacles, the same as the other piece was. Well, I checked with *another* oculist, and *he* says you were right. Remember you weren't at all certain that it was from the same—"

"Never mind that," Mason interrupted. "What's the latest?"

"It's a pretty small sliver to check on, Perry. That first man was afraid to say it wasn't Hardisty's because the sheriff had the big chunk, and said it was. . . . Well, anyway, I've stumbled onto an oculist who has made some very delicate and complete tests. He says this piece isn't from Hardisty's spectacles, but that the piece the sheriff has is made to Hardisty's prescription. That means there were *two* broken spectacles.

"Now, according to this oculist, the normal eye has a certain power of adjustment, or what is known as accommodation. It's really an ability to change the thickness of the lens of the eyeball, which has the effect of bringing objects into focus—just the same as you move the lens of a camera in and out, in order to focus it on some object."

Mason nodded.

"That power is lost as a person becomes older. At the age of about forty, a person needs bifocals; at about sixty, he loses the power of accommodation altogether. Of course, some persons are more immune to the effects of age so far as the eye is concerned, but on a general average, an optician can tell the age of a person pretty well from the correction of his eyeglass. Now, this oculist tells me that just making a guess—not something he'd be willing to swear to under oath, but making a darned close guess—that the spectacle lens came from the glasses of a person just about thirty-six years old.

"Now, Jack Hardisty was thirty-two. Milicent Hardisty

is twenty-seven, Adele is twenty-five. Harley Raymand is twenty-five, Vincent Blane is fifty-two, Rodney Beaton is about thirty-five, but he doesn't wear any glasses. He's one of those chaps who have perfect eyes. . . . But here's something you haven't considered. Myrna Payson seems to be thirty or so, but she *may* be a lot older. She doesn't ordinarily wear glasses, but she may wear 'em when she's reading—or when she's checking astronomical time in connection with a buried clock."

Mason flung himself into his big creaking swivel chair. He melted back in the chair, rested his head against the cushioned back, closed his eyes, then said abruptly, "Done anything about it, Paul?"

Drake shook his head. "The idea just occurred to me. Somehow I hadn't considered her in connection with those glasses and the clock."

"Consider her now, then," Mason said without opening his eyes.

"I'm going to," Drake said, getting to his feet. "I'm starting right now. Is there anything else?"

"Nothing else," Mason said. "Only we've got to tie up that sidereal time angle tight by tomorrow morning. I think McNair is going to throw the case into my lap sometime tomorrow. Then I'll have to start putting on evidence. I haven't any to put on. The only thing I can do is to use that clock to inject such an element of mystery into the case that McNair will have to take notice of it."

"Can't you do that anyway?" Drake asked.

"Not unless I can get the clock introduced into evidence," Mason said, "and how I'm going to prove that sidereal time has anything to do with the murder of Jack Hardisty, is beyond me. The more I cudgel my mind on it, the more I find myself running around in circles."

Drake started for the door. "Okay," he said, "I'm going up and do a little snooping around Myrna Payson's cattle ranch."

"Watch out for her," Della Street said, laughing. "She oozes sex appeal."

Drake said, "Sex appeal means nothing to me."

"So I've noticed," Della Street observed.

Drake had reached the door when he paused, took a wallet from his pocket, opened it and said, "I've got something else here, Perry. I don't think it has a darn thing to do with the case, but I found it out there by the rock, not over twenty-five yards from where the clock was first found. . . . See what you make of it."

Drake opened an envelope he took from the wallet, and handed Mason a small circular piece of black paper, not quite the size of a silver dollar.

Mason inspected it, a puzzled frown drawing his eyebrows together. "It seems to be a circle carefully cut from a piece of brand-new carbon paper."

"That's it," Drake agreed, and "that's all of it. You can't make another darn thing out of it."

Mason said, "The circle was carefully drawn. You can see where the point of a compass made a little hole here. Then the circle was drawn and cut with the greatest care. The carbon paper had evidently never been used, otherwise there'd be lines on it or the imprint of type."

"Exactly," Drake agreed. "Evidently someone wanted to make a tracing of something, but never used the circular bit of paper—it's about the size of a small watch. It probably doesn't mean a darn thing, Perry, but I found it lying there and thought I'd better bring it along."

"Thanks, Paul. Glad you did. It may check up with something later."

Paul Drake said, "Well, I'll be on my way. Be seeing you."

Mason remained tilted back in the swivel chair for nearly five minutes after Paul Drake had left, then he straightened himself, drummed his fingers on the edge of the desk for a few moments, then shook his head.

"What's the matter?" Della Street asked.

"It doesn't click," Mason said. "It just doesn't fit. The clock, the glasses, the stars, the—" Abruptly Mason broke off. He frowned, and half closed his right eye, staring fixedly at the far wall of the room.

"What is it?" Della Street asked.

"Martha Stevens," Mason said slowly.

"What about her?"

"She's thirty-eight."

"I don't get you."

"Thirty-eight," Mason said, "wears spectacles. A practical nurse, trained in the giving of hypodermics, because she gives Vincent Blane his insulin shots. . . . *Now*, do you get it?"

"Heavens, yes!"

"And," Mason went on, "the night after the murder when Adele Blane disappeared, she went to the San Venito Hotel and registered as Martha Stevens. . . . We never found out why."

"Do you know now?" Della asked breathlessly.

Mason said, "I know what *might* have been a reason."

"What?"

"Martha Stevens had a date with someone at the San Venito Hotel. She couldn't keep it. Adele went there and registered under the name of Martha Stevens, so she could meet whatever person was to call on Martha Stevens."

"Who?" Della asked.

Mason hesitated for a moment, drumming with his fingers on the edge of the desk. Abruptly he picked up the telephone, and gave Vincent Blane's number in Kenvale.

After a few minutes, he said, "Hello. Who is this speaking please? Oh, yes, Mrs. Stevens. . . . Is anyone

194

home except you? . . . I see. Well, Mr. Blane wanted you to take his hypodermic syringe—the one he uses on his insulin shots—to the office of the Drake Detective Agency. You can just leave it here. He wanted you to catch the first interurban bus and bring it in. Do you think you can do that? . . . Yes, right away. . . . No, I don't know, Mrs. Stevens. All I know is that's what Mr. Blane asked me to notify you. He's feeling rather upset—the strain of the trial and all—yes, I understand. Thank you. Good-by."

Della Street looked at him curiously. "What good does that do?" she asked.

Mason pulled open a drawer in his desk, took out a bunch of skeleton keys.

"It gives us an opportunity to go through the room of Martha Stevens, and do a little searching along lines that probably haven't occurred to the police. . . . And perhaps steal a pair of glasses."

"That comes under the head of burglarious housebreaking?" Della Street asked.

Mason grinned. "In view of the fact that I'm employed by the owner of the house, and might be considered to have his implied permission, there's a technical question as to the burglarious intent."

"Would the district attorney appreciate such a technicality?"

"I'm afraid he wouldn't. Hamilton Burger, the district attorney, or Thomas L. McNair, the brilliant trial deputy, would hardly think there was anything to differentiate the act from burglary—*if I got caught.*"

"Can't you get the evidence in the regular way?"

"There isn't time. If I can find some peg on which to hang the evidence of that clock, I've got to know about it tonight. And if I can't find anything, the sooner I know that, the sooner I can start on some other approach."

195

Della Street walked over to the cloak closet and took her hat down from the shelf.

"Where," Mason asked, "do you think *you're* going?"

"Along."

Mason grinned. "Okay. Come on."

25

Vincent Blane's house went back to an ancient day of architecture when huge frame houses garnished with gables, ornamental half turrets and balconies sprawled over spacious grounds, in an era of tranquillity, financial security and happiness.

Mason surveyed the big spaciousness of the house. "I presume," he said, "it will be one of the rooms in the back."

"Probably on the ground floor," Della said. "Let's try the back door first."

"No," Mason said. "The back door will be locked from the inside, and have the key in it. The front door will have a nightlatch. We can work it with one of these passkeys—if we're lucky."

They waited until the street was deserted, then slipped up to the dark porch. Della Street held a small fountain-pen flashlight while Mason ran through his bunch of skeleton keys, looking for the right one.

"Here's where we give another statute a compound fracture," Della Street said. "I was afraid our law-abiding rôle was getting too irksome."

Mason selected a key he thought might do the work, and

196

inserted it tentatively in the lock. "We're doing it in an emergency to clear a client who may be innocent."

"If she's innocent," Della Street said spitefully, "why doesn't she tell you the true story of what happened?"

"Because she's afraid to. The truth looks too black. She—" The lock clicked back in the middle of the explanation. Mason opened the door, grinned and said, "Did it with the first key. That's an omen, Della."

The house was warm, with an aura of human occupancy. There was a comfortable, lived-in aroma clinging to the rooms, the faint after-smell of good cigars and well-seasoned cooking—the mellow feeling which clings to huge wooden houses and is almost never found in fireproof apartments.

Mason said, "Okay, we'll head for the back of the house. There are back stairs. I remember seeing them that day when the officers came to get Milicent Hardisty."

Della Street said, "Her room might be at the head of the back stairs. At any rate, it'll be a good place to start."

Within five minutes they had found it. A room on the second floor, at the extreme back of the house.

"It's pretty hard to make a search with flashlights," Della Street said.

Mason nodded, boldly walked over to the light switch, and clicked it on. "Neighbors," he announced, "get suspicious when they see the beam of a flashlight playing around a room, or even impinging against the drawn shades, but they think nothing of it when lights are on. . . . Just make certain the shades are all drawn, Della."

Della Street went around the room pulling shades.

"All right," Mason said, "let's get to work."

"What are we searching for?" Della Street asked.

197

Mason grinned. "That's the beauty of it. We don't know, we—" He broke off abruptly. "What was that, Della?"

Della Street said, "Someone tossed gravel up against the window."

Mason frowned. "Sit tight. See what happens."

A moment later more gravel was thrown against the window.

"Do I dare to switch out the lights, and take a peek at whoever is below?" Della asked.

Mason thought for a moment, then said, "Give it a try, Della."

He switched out the lights. Della Street drew back the window shades, stood against the dark window, looking down into the back yard.

After a moment she moved back from the window and said with an odd catch in her voice, "It's a man. He beckoned to me, and then moved up to the back porch. He's standing there waiting, as though expecting me to let him in."

For a long moment Mason deliberated this new development, then he said with sudden decision, "Okay, Della. We let him in."

"But we can't afford to be caught here, and—"

"We let him in," Mason repeated. "It's a hunch. Maybe Martha Stevens' boy friend. . . . Come on, Della, unlock the back door, and don't say a word. I'll be standing directly behind you. See what he does."

With the aid of the flashlight, they negotiated the back stairs, crossed the kitchen. Della Street unlocked the back door, Mason switched out the flashlight, stood directly behind her. As the door opened, a slender man, wearing a reefer-type overcoat, pushed his way into the room and slipped a familiar arm around Della Street's waist. "Cripes," he said, "thought I wasn't going to get away. Give us a kiss."

Mason's flashlight snapped on.

The man frowned at the annoyance of the flashlight, then caught a glimpse of Della Street's face and jumped back as though he'd been shot. "Say, what's the idea?" he demanded.

Mason said with every assurance of authority, "Come on up," he invited.

"Where to?"

"Martha's room."

"Say, who do you think *you* are?"

Mason said with every assurance of authority. "Come along, my man, I want you to answer questions about what happened the night Jack Hardisty was murdered."

Every bit of resistance oozed out of the man as though he had been hit hard in the solar plexus. "Who . . . who *are* you?" he asked, his shoulders drooping, the coat seeming suddenly much too large.

Mason merely clasped an authoritative hand on the man's arm. "Come on."

Silently they climbed the stairs, entered Martha Stevens' room. Accusingly, Mason turned to regard the frightened man. He fixed him with a steady, penetrating scrutiny that he used at times effectively in his cross-examination.

"All right," he said, at length. "Let's have it."

"Where's Martha?"

Mason said, "Martha's having a chance to tell her story to a Los Angeles detective. You can tell yours *now*."

The man fidgeted uneasily. "I haven't done anything."

Mason merely smiled.

The man settled down in a chair, his body seemingly trying to hide behind the heavy folds of the sagging coat.

Mason said, "We haven't got all night. . . . What's your name?"

"William Smiley."

"Where were you," Mason asked, "when Martha Stevens broke her glasses?"

199

"I was right there."

"How did they get broken?"

"This guy lunged at her."

"You mean Hardisty?"

"Yes."

Della Street quietly extracted a notebook from her purse, unscrewed the cap from a small fountain pen, and started making shorthand hieroglyphics.

"Why did you go up to the cabin to meet Hardisty in the first place?" Mason asked.

"It was Martha's idea. She'd been reading the dope in this magazine about how this drug made people talk. Hardisty had been dipping into funds, and Blane was going to have to make good, so Martha figured that by giving him a shot of this drug, we could make him talk his head off, and get the money back.

"She knew she was going to have to use force. That's where I came in. . . . I didn't like it. I didn't want to. She'll tell you that herself."

"I know," Mason said sympathetically, glancing from the corner of his eye to see that Della Street was keeping up with the conversation. "Just tell me what happened, so that I can check it with Martha's story."

"Martha won't lie, she'll tell you the truth."

"I know," Mason said soothingly.

"Martha and I would have married, only Blane doesn't want a married housekeeper. He always said he never hired a couple that was any good. Either the man was good and the woman wasn't, or the other way around. . . . Well, Martha and I was going together secret-like. This thing came up, and she called on me."

"Where did you get the hypodermic?" Mason asked.

"One she used to give Blane his shots for diabetes."

Mason waited for the other to go on.

Smiley, recalling what had happened, became less hostile. "Okay," he said in a nasal, somewhat whining voice as though he were accustomed to registering complaints which did no good, "what was there for *me* to do? I had to go through with it. Martha got the gun for me."

"What kind of a gun?" Mason asked with a significant glance at Della Street.

"A thirty-eight. It was Mrs. Hardisty's gun. Mrs. Hardisty was spending part of the time over here. She kept that gun in her suitcase. Martha got it and gave it to me. We went up to the cabin. Hardisty was there, all right. He'd parked his car and was standing right by this big granite rock. He had a spade in his hands, like he was going to dig. I wanted to try talking with Hardisty, to be reasonable about it, but Martha was all business. She gave him the works right away."

"Shot him?" Mason asked.

"No. Don't be silly! *I* had the gun. She told him she was going to give him this hypo, that it would make him tell the truth, and not to try getting rough. I cut down on him with the gun, and made him get his hands up. He was scared, but not *too* scared."

"And what did Martha do?"

"She gave him the hypo."

"And then what?"

"Then, I guess he came to the conclusion that I wouldn't shoot. Anyway he made a swing at Martha, and clipped her one that knocked off her glasses, and it gave her a jolt."

"And you shot?" Mason asked.

"Not me, brother. I got sore when he pasted Martha. I hauled off and hit him."

"With the hand that was holding the gun?"

"No. I tossed the gun away when I pasted him. . . . Damn little shrimp, hitting a woman. I should have broken his jaw. As it was, I knocked him down and he broke his glasses—we thought we'd picked up all the pieces. Guess we missed some."

"And then what happened?" Mason asked.

"He wouldn't talk for a while, then finally he got to talking. At first I thought that magazine article was on the up-and-up. He said he was just about ready to call the whole thing off and go to Blane and make a clean breast of it. He said that he didn't have the nerve for a job like that, that every time he hid the stuff he was afraid the police would find it. He said he'd hid it in his house first. Then he'd got nervous and gone up to the tunnel with it, buried it in the end of the old mining tunnel. That had been only an hour or so ago, but he'd got nervous before he'd driven half a mile and began thinking of other and better places. He said after he'd hidden the stuff in the tunnel it seemed like any school kid would have picked the tunnel as a place to look.

"Of course, it's easy to look back now and see what this guy was doing to us. Martha had made the mistake of telling him this drug was going to make him tell the truth. Maybe it would have if we'd given it a chance, but he out-foxed us. He pretended it had taken effect before he even felt it, and sent us on a wild-goose chase."

"You mean you went to the tunnel?" Mason asked.

"Sure. We fell for it, hook, line and sinker. We left him there at the rock, and Martha and I went up to the tunnel. We took his spade along to dig with."

"And you dug?"

"I'll say we dug. I haven't shoveled so much dirt in a year—and the lousy crook had the swag right there in his car all the time. He just outsmarted us, that's all."

"What did you do when you realized he'd been lying to you?" Mason asked.

"We came back to see if we could question him some more. Naturally, we couldn't find him. He'd dusted out, lock, stock and barrel, as soon as he got rid of us. So then we came on back home."

"Exactly where was it that you met Hardisty?"

"Right by that big granite rock. He was there with the spade. Looked like he was getting ready to do some digging. If we'd only laid low we could have caught him red-handed. It was this hypo that queered things, gave him his chance to slip one over on us."

"And this was before dark?"

"Sure. It was late in the afternoon, but it was light, all right."

"While you were driving up, did you meet Adele Blane on the road?"

"She drove right past us just before we made the turn off to the cabin," Smiley said, "but she didn't see us. She had some fellow with her."

"Did you see anything of a clock that was buried near that—"

"Nope," Smiley interrupted. "I read about that buried clock. It doesn't make sense to me. Why would Hardisty want to bury a clock?"

For a long moment there was silence, then Mason said, "You came back to this house with Martha Stevens?"

"Nope. We were afraid there might be a kickback on that dope business. She put me on the interurban. I went in to Los Angeles. She was to meet me there the next night at a hotel. She'd registered, all right, but she went out again and didn't come back. I called there and hung around for a while, but she never did show up."

"And you didn't go back to recover your gun?" Mason asked.

"No. I just chucked it away when he hung one on Martha. Then after I got him licked and he got started talking, I forgot all about the gun. As soon as he said he'd buried the stuff in the tunnel, Martha and I fell for it. We beat it up there. I did want to take him with us, but he acted dopey and just sat down all caved-in like, and his eyes got glassy. Martha pushed the spade at me

203

and said to come on, that she knew where the tunnel was. . . . Shucks, the guy had never been near the tunnel. I tell you he had the dough right there in the car with him."

"Did you go into the cabin when you got back from the tunnel?" Mason asked.

"No. We saw Jack Hardisty's car was gone, so we took it for granted he'd beat it. We left the spade up there, got in our car and came back."

"How long were you up at the tunnel?"

"I don't know, maybe an hour and a half from the time we left until we got back. It was pretty dark when we got back to the cabin."

"How did it happen you didn't pick up the gun, if you picked up the broken glasses?"

"We picked up the glasses right after the fight. You know how a person picks up glasses as soon as they get broken. Martha was picking up pieces of glass almost as soon as he'd knocked 'em off."

"Who picked up his glasses?"

"I did. I put 'em in my pocket. There was just one big piece knocked out of his. I was afraid to give 'em to him, sort of afraid they might be evidence."

"And you knew the gun was found later on?"

"Oh, sure. I read the papers about the trail and all that, and Martha's told me stuff. . . . How come Martha hasn't told you this?"

"Where were you working?" Mason asked.

"Turret Construction Company—defense work. Been there for six months."

"You read in the papers about Hardisty's body being discovered in the cabin?"

"Sure."

"Do you know whether he was in the cabin when you got back from the tunnel?"

"No I don't. His car was gone—and I was getting an

awful case of cold feet. You know, jabbing a man full of a drug—"

"I know. Where did Martha get this drug, do you know?"

"She told Mrs. Hardisty she wanted to get it. I don't know what excuse it was she gave to Mrs. Hardisty, or what she said she wanted it for. I think she told Mrs. Hardisty the old man wanted it, or intended to use it, somehow. . . . Anyhow, Mrs. Hardisty was friendly with a doctor, and she said she could get it. I don't think Hardisty's own wife even knew he was short. Martha found out about it listening to Blane talking on the long distance phone with the bank directors over at Roxbury."

Mason said abruptly, "You haven't told anyone anything about this?"

"No."

"Not a soul?"

"Not a soul."

Mason said, "Well, I think Martha Stevens will be home pretty quick. You can wait here, if you want."

"Not me. I don't like to come in the house unless Martha's here. I don't think the old man would like it. I saw the light up here and threw a little gravel against the window pane. That's our signal. . . . I'll go out and wait around outside, until Martha gets here. You don't think it will be long?"

"No, I don't think it will be long," Mason said.

Della Street closed her notebook, dropped it into her bag, screwed the cap on the fountain pen, glanced at Perry Mason. He shook his head, almost imperceptibly.

The three of them walked out of the house. Mason said, "Well, good night, Smiley."

"Good night, sir."

Mason helped Della Street into the automobile.

"Couldn't you have used him somehow?" she asked in a low voice.

205

Mason said, "If he ever told that story in front of a jury, Mrs. Hardisty would be out of the frying pan and into the fire. This is one of those cases where they throw everything at you except the kitchen sink. . . . You can begin to understand now why Milicent is keeping her mouth shut, why Dr. Macon doesn't dare to say a word. Dr. Macon thinks she did it."

"Are you sure?"

"It's a cinch," Mason said. "Remember, she went to him for the scopolamine. Remember, she was a trained nurse before she was married. Dr. Macon thought she wanted to try this drug on Jack Hardisty. Evidently there'd been a magazine article on it. . . . He probably thinks Milicent is lying to protect her father as well as herself."

"But if they had Milicent's gun, what gun was it that she threw away?"

Mason said, "It wasn't what *she* threw away, it was what *I* threw away."

"How do you mean?"

"The only point I had to argue to a jury," Mason went on, "was that *if* Milicent Hardisty had thrown her gun down an embankment, that same gun couldn't very well have been found beside the big granite rock. . . . I couldn't keep my big mouth shut. I had to take what seemed to be a minor discrepancy at the time, and use it to heckle Jameson. Now Jameson is up there searching for that gun, and if he finds it—Well, if he finds it, we're not only licked, we're crucified—unless I can figure out some way I can get that damned clock introduced in evidence."

"Well, there's one thing," Della said. "You know what happened now."

Mason's eyes were thoughtful. "I'm not so certain that I do."

"What do you mean by that? That Smiley was lying?"

206

Mason said, "One bit of evidence bothers me."

"What?"

"Hardisty's trousers. The red clay mud showed that he *had* been up at the tunnel—and someone took off his shoes, removed every bit of mud on the shoes, polished them, put them by the bed—and forgot to inspect the cuffs on his trousers."

Della Street's eyes were wide. "Then . . . then Smiley must have been lying?"

"Or telling the exact, unvarnished truth," Mason said.

26

Thomas McNair seemed more debonair than ever as he took his seat in court the next morning. The crowded courtroom buzzed with whispered conversation. The jurors solemnly filed in and took their seats. And then, Hamilton Burger himself, a barrel-chested figure whose every movement suggested a bulldog tenacity, entered the courtroom and took his seat beside McNair.

Mason knew they were moving in for the kill. They'd rush the case to a quick, unexpected conclusion, and then toss it into his lap, let him try floundering around, searching for a weak link in the chain of circumstantial evidence which gripped the defendants.

Deputy sheriffs escorted the defendants into the courtroom. Dr. Macon, with his face set in a fixed mask to conceal his feelings, seated himself with motions that were stiff with self-discipline. Milicent Hardisty dropped into her chair, almost immediately propped an elbow on the arm of the chair, and rested her head against the upraised hand. Her attitude was that of tired dejection. She only wanted to get it over with as soon as possible.

Judge Canfield emerged from his chambers. The people in the courtroom arose as with one motion. After the judge seated himself, a gavel pounded counsel and spectators back to their seats.

"People *versus* Macon and Hardisty," Judge Canfield said with a crisp, businesslike efficiency. "Both defendants are in court, and the jurors are all present, gentlemen. Proceed with the case."

McNair went nimbly ahead producing witnesses who identified the molds of tire tracks which had been found at the Blane cabin, then expert witnesses who testified as to the make of the tires which had made those tracks, testified to checking the molds against the tires on Dr. Macon's car.

And then Hamilton Burger, the district attorney, took over with ponderous dignity, with the lumbering efficiency of a big-gunned battle wagon swinging into action. "We wish to recall William N. Jameson," he said.

Jameson, looking slightly weary about the eyes, but full of spirit, took the stand.

"You have already been sworn," the district attorney rumbled. "Now, Mr. Jameson, I am going to direct your attention to the fact that yesterday on cross-examination, counsel asked you if you had made any search of the spot near where the defendant, Milicent Hardisty, had been standing when she was seen by witnesses to throw a gun, or an object resembling a gun, into a canyon. And you testified, I believe, that you had made no such search."

"That is correct."

"Do you now wish to change that testimony?"

"Not the testimony. At the time I answered the question, my testimony was correct, but since then I've made a very careful and exhaustive search of the locality."

"When was that search made?"

"Last night."

"When did it start?"

"At about six o'clock."

"When did it terminate?"

"At about two-thirty this morning."

"Why did you terminate your search?"

"Because I found the object for which I was looking."

"Did you indeed! And what was that object?"

"A thirty-eight caliber Colt, police positive, double-action revolver, with all six chambers loaded, the gun bearing the number one-four-five-eight-one, and also bearing thereon two somewhat smudged latent fingerprints, which however, are readily identifiable as the fingerprints of the defendant, Milicent Hardisty."

Hamilton Burger was too dignified to smirk triumphantly at Perry Mason as McNair would have done. He said simply, "Your witness, Mr. Mason."

"No questions," Mason snapped.

Hamilton Burger seemed somewhat surprised. However, he promptly called a representative of the sheriff's office, who testified that some five years ago an application had been duly made by a citizen of Kenvale to carry a concealed weapon for the purpose of protection. The weapon was described as the Colt police positive, thirty-eight caliber, double-action revolver, bearing the number 14581.

"You have that application with you?"

"I have."

"Did any person witness the signing of that application?"

"Yes, sir. I did."

"It was signed in your presence?"

"It was."

"And I will ask you who signed that application?"

"Mr. Vincent P. Blane," the witness said, and then

added gratuitously, "the father of the defendant, Milicent Hardisty."

Hamilton Burger moved with the slow dignity of a steam roller as he got up and walked over to the witness. "I will now ask that this application to carry a firearm be received in evidence as an exhibit on behalf of the People, and marked by the clerk with the appropriate exhibit number."

Judge Canfield glanced at Perry Mason. "Any objection on the part of the defendant, Hardisty, Mr. Mason?"

Mason managed a bold front for the jurors. "None whatever," he said.

Hamilton Burger said with that ponderous manner which was so characteristic of him, "Your Honor, I would like to recall Rodney Beaton for a few questions. I think the Court will appreciate the position in which the prosecution finds itself. Due to the finding of this second weapon, the finding of the so-called first weapon, or prosecution's exhibit A, becomes relatively more important. . . . That is, the circumstances surrounding the finding assume an added significance."

Judge Canfield said, "The court will permit you to recall the witness, Counselor."

Burger bowed his head gravely. "Rodney Beaton, come forward, please."

Rodney Beaton arose from his position near the back of the courtroom, advanced to the witness stand.

Once more it was Hamilton Burger, himself, who did the questioning. "Mr. Beaton, you have previously been interrogated concerning the finding of a weapon which has been produced in evidence as the People's exhibit A. I call your attention, Mr. Beaton, to that exhibit, and also to the fact that the cartridge in one of the cylinders has been discharged. I'm going to ask you if, when you and Miss Lola Strague found that weapon, you no-

210

ticed anything in connection with that discharged cartridge?"

Beaton said, "I noticed that it had been freshly fired."

Burger shook his head. "That is a conclusion. You are not, I take it, an expert on firearms?"

Beaton smiled. "I think I am."

Burger showed some surprise. "What has been your experience?"

"I've been a collector of firearms for several years. I held a State championship as a revolver shot for two consecutive years. I have shot thousands of rounds in revolvers of different types. I have studied the effects of different loads, different shapes and weights of cartridges, both by consulting the available data of firearm and cartridge manufacturers, as well as by practical observations of my own."

Hamilton Burger's face showed great satisfaction, "And as a result of your knowledge, do I undestand you to say that this weapon had been recently fired?"

"Within twenty-four hours," Beaton said positively.

"How can you tell?"

"By the smell of powder fumes in the barrel. There's a certain subtle change in odor after a weapon is fired. For the first few hours there's a decided acrid odor, which later gives way to a more metallic smell."

"Now, you have pointed out on the map, People's exhibit C, the approximate spot where this weapon was found. Can you state anything in connection with the physical appearance of the ground?"

Beaton said carefully, "The weapon, when Miss Strague and I found it, was lying in some pine needles, which in turn were on a rather soft stretch of ground. The weapon was indented in the ground, as though it has been stepped on."

"Were there any marks of struggle?"

"The pine needles would not hold clear-cut footprints,

211

but there was a certain scuffing of the pine needles in the immediate vicinity. I'm accustomed to studying tracks in connection with my photographic activities. A deer in deep pine needles will leave a certain scuffed-up track, and I thought for a while these were deer tracks, but I changed my mind when—"

"Never mind your conclusions, Mr. Beaton. Simply state the physical appearance of the pine needles."

"Well, they were scuffed up."

"You may cross-examine," Burger said to Perry Mason.

"What brought you to this particular place," Mason asked, "at the time you discovered the gun?"

"Miss Strague and I were prospecting for a camera location. For some time I had been planning to set up one of my camera traps at a spot immediately to the south and west of the granite outcropping. A careful study of the tracks of animals, however, convinced me at the last minute that there was a better location for the camera to the south and east of this rock outcropping."

"At approximately the point where the weapon was discovered?"

"Yes, sir. I was making a survey there, preparatory to placing the camera there."

"And previously you had made a survey of the point to the south and west?"

"That's right."

"And on this particular occasion, when you and Miss Strague found this weapon, you took notice of the tracks, Mr. Beaton?"

"Yes, sir."

"And you state that you have made it a point to notice tracks?"

"Yes, sir. I consider myself something of a naturalist. In getting night photographs of nocturnal animals, one must necessarily place cameras with some degree of skill —at least if first-class photographs are to result."

"During the time that you were making a survey of this locality, did you see any clock, or did you hear the ticking of any clock, or did you—"

Hamilton Burger was up on his feet, clearing his throat importantly as he arose. "Your Honor," he interrupted, "it seems that—no, Your Honor, pardon me Counselor, finish the question."

"Or," Mason asked, "did you notice any indication that the ground had been disturbed in any way?"

"Your Honor," Hamilton Burger said, "this is objected to as incompetent, irrelevant and immaterial, as not proper cross-examination. If the defendants wish to get any evidence concerning a clock into this case, it will be necessary for them to introduce it on their *own* case and as part of that case. Furthermore, it appears that an attempt at this time to drag an alarm clock into this case, and to enshroud it with some sinister significance, is merely an attempt to confuse the issues and the jurors. I challenge counsel to point out to the court at this time any possible theory on which this clock can have anything to do with the murder of Jack Hardisty."

Burger sat down.

Mason smiled and said, "At this time, Your Honor, I am only cross-examining the witness to test his recollection, and to determine the nature and extent of the search he made at that time."

"As cross-examination directed for that purpose, the question will be permitted, and the objection is overruled," Judge Canfield said.

"No, sir. I saw no sign of any buried clock, I heard no ticking of any clock. I saw no indication that the ground had been disturbed."

"Subsequently, Mr. Beaton, while you were on the

213

ground, did you have any of the witnesses point out to you a spot at which a clock had been found?"

Both Hamilton Burger and Thomas McNair were on their feet. It was Thomas McNair, forceful, dramatic, rapid in his conversation, who managed to get the first objection into the record. "Your Honor, we object. That is absolutely incompetent. It is an attempt to drag another issue into this case. It calls for hearsay evidence. It is an attempt to prove an incompetent fact by asking a witness about a conversation."

Hamilton Burger cleared his throat, added importantly, "It is a matter which has, at no time, been touched upon in direct examination, Your Honor. No claim is made that the question even relates to the same general locality, concerning which the witness testified."

Judge Canfield nodded his head. "It would seem that this objection is well taken, Counselor," he said to Mason.

"I would like to be heard upon it, Your Honor."

"Very well."

Mason looked at the clock. "This, Your Honor, is a crucial point in the case. I think, if the Court please, I can get some authorities on the matter if I am given a little time. After all, some of the events of the morning, while known in advance to the district attorney, have naturally taken the defense entirely by surprise. The Court will note that this testimony about the second gun is at complete variance to the situation as heretofore disclosed by the testimony."

"But that was outlined, anticipated and even suggested in your cross-examination yesterday, Mr. Mason."

There was a smile in Mason's eyes as he said, "And the witness offered to bet me a million dollars there was no second weapon to be found in that barranca. In the absence of the million-dollar payment, I should be entitled to sufficient time to investigate the new legal situation disclosed by this abrupt switch in the testimony."

"Very well," Judge Canfield said, smiling. "Court will take a recess until two o'clock this afternoon. If you wish to look up authorities, Mr. Mason, please bear in mind the point made by the prosecution, that this is an attempt to prove an extraneous fact by hearsay evidence. Not only does the Court consider the fact itself to be extraneous and irrelevant, but the question, as framed, called upon the witness to relate some action he had taken in connection with a statement made by some other person."

"But Your Honor will note," Mason said, "that the question relates to an activity *on the part of this witness.* The *reason* for that activity is embodied as a part of the question. I think we are entitled to show the activity, and, having shown that, the reason for it, as it might tend to show bias on the part of the witness."

Judge Canfield frowned thoughtfully, then shook his head.

Hamilton Burger said, "If the Court please—"

"The Court will recess until two o'clock," Judge Canfield said, "and all arguments will be heard at that time. In the meantime, there is nothing to be gained by a further discussion. However, the Court will consider that it is incumbent upon Mr. Mason to produce authorities in support of his question. Failing in that, the objection will be sustained. I think that clarifies the situation and the position of the Court. We will recess until two o'clock."

27

Back in his office, Mason held a hurried conference with Jackson, his law clerk, Della Street and Paul Drake.

"Find me some authority," he said to Jack, "which even squints at the doctrine that hearsay evidence may be brought out on cross-examination to show the *reason* which actuated the witness. . . . There *must* be some authority somewhere—such, for instance, as a question, Didn't you go to a certain place, because so-and-so told you that such-and-such was the case?"

Jackson nodded, vanished into the law library.

Mason, frowning, said, "Unless I can drag that clock in on cross-examination, I'm not going to get it in. And the way things look right now, I'm not going to get it in on cross-examination."

"Did you think you could?" Della Street asked.

Mason said, "I'm sparring for time. Burger intended to rest his case. Judge Canfield would then have given me until two o'clock to put on my case. As it is now, we'll start arguing at two o'clock. I can talk for ten or fifteen minutes. Then let's suppose Judge Canfield rules against me, and *then* Burger rests his case. The Judge will then give me another continuance until tomorrow morning before I have to start putting on my case. I'll gain that much. . . . Damn it, Paul, that clock means something, and yet I can't even get it into evidence unless I can find out *what* it means."

"We can't get anywhere with Mrs. Payson," Drake said. "She's interested in astrology, but she's interested in a lot of other things. Astrology, it seems, doesn't have so much to do with astronomy, and like lots of women who talk about the signs of the zodiac, she doesn't know a damn thing about the stars themselves."

"You're certain?"

"Yes. I've pumped her."

"She might have been holding out on you."

"I don't think so."

Mason said, "Hang it, Paul. That clock wasn't set on sidereal time just as an accident. It wasn't—" He broke off abruptly.

"What's the matter?" Drake asked.

Mason said, "An idea, that's all . . . but— shucks, Paul!"

Mason picked up the telephone, said to the girl at the switchboard, "Gertie, get me the county clerk's office. I want the deputy who has charge of exhibits in the case of People *versus* Hardisty and Macon. I'll wait on the phone."

Mason held the telephone, his fingertips drumming the desk. After a few moments he said, "Hello. This is Perry Mason talking. That alarm clock which was introduced into evidence . . . Is it still running? It is. How fast is it running? . . . Check that accurately, will you? Let me have the exact time shown on it at a certain precise moment."

Mason took out his watch, laid it on the desk in front of him, said, "Okay, let me have it right now."

He marked down the figures on a pad of paper, frowned thoughtfully at them, then said after a moment, "Yes, that's all. Thank you."

He dropped the receiver back into place, said, "That's strange."

"What is?" Della Street asked.

"In the first place," Mason said, "that's a twenty-four-hour clock. We can count on somewhere around thirty-six hours to a winding. It will vary somewhat, depending upon the condition of the spring and the make of the clock. However, it's still running strong. That indicated it was wound up shortly before it was discovered. But the interesting thing is that *the clock hasn't gained a minute since yesterday."*

"Well?" Della Street asked.

"Sidereal time," Mason said, "is almost exactly four minutes faster each day. It lacks just two or three seconds of that. It—" Abruptly he threw back his head and began to laugh.

"What is it?" Della Street asked.

Mason's laughter became uproarious. "The joke," he said, "is on me. I'm laughing at myself. We baited a trap and then walked into it ourselves."

"I don't get you," Drake said.

Mason said, "It goes back to the quotation about the engineer being hoist with his own petard. . . . Della, tell Jackson not to make any further investigation. We won't need those authorities. . . . Now give me half an hour to get my thoughts straightened out and we'll walk into court and give Mr. Hamilton Burger and his fresh assistant, Mr. Thomas L. McNair, a jolt they'll remember as long as they live! The solution of this whole mystery has been staring me right in the face, and I've been so blind I couldn't see it!"

28

It was five minutes past two, and Judge Canfield glanced down at Perry Mason. "Are you ready to submit authorities in support of your position, Counselor?"

Mason smiled. "No, Your Honor. I've decided to abandon my position. I will withdraw my question."

Hamilton Burger plainly showed his surprise. McNair sneered openly. "Very well," Judge Canfield said without giving any indication of his feelings, "Proceed."

"Just a few more questions of the witness," Mason said. "Mr. Beaton, you have testified that you are an expert tracker."

"Well, not exactly, but I have given considerable attention to the study of tracks."

"Yes. And you have set up several cameras at various points of vantage in the vicinity of your cabin, and in the vicinity of the Blane cabin where this murder was committed?"

"Yes, sir."

"Referring back, Mr. Beaton, to the time when the witness Jameson discovered Dr. Macon at the Blane cabin. You were there at that time?"

"Yes, sir."

"Prior to that time, where had you been?"

"I had been out watching my cameras, making the rounds, as I call it."

"Alone?"

"No. Miss Strague was with me."

"And Burton Strague, Miss Strague's brother, subsequently joined you at the cabin?"

"That's right."

"And stated he'd been looking for you all over the mountain and that his search had been fruitless?"

"Yes."

"And further stated that he'd walked through one of your camera traps, in connection with that search?"

"Yes."

"And told you which camera it was?"

"Yes, sir."

"And what was the time that he said he walked through that trap?"

"I don't know if he said. I know what time it was, however, because I made a notation when the flashbulb exploded."

"You were where you could see it explode?"

"Yes, sir. I saw the flare of light."

"And you customarily note such times?"

"You mean make notations of the time the lights flare up?"

"Yes."

"Yes, sir, I do."

"And yet, when it came to fixing the time when you saw the defendant, Milicent Hardisty, throwing a gun away, you weren't able to fix it very accurately, were you?"

The witness smiled. "My watches, Mr. Mason, are set sometimes by guess. When I make a note of the time a picture is taken, I do it for my own convenience, not because the standard time makes any difference. It is only the relative time. In other words, I wish the data for my own files. I want to know the relative time. That is, how long after the camera was set, before it was exposed, and things of that sort."

"Yes," Mason said, "so that your watch may at times be as much as half an hour off standard time?"

"I would say so, yes."

Mason said, "Now, did you develop the picture that was taken when Burton Strague walked through the camera trap?"

Again Beaton smiled, "I did, yes, sir."

"You don't happen to have a print of that picture with you, do you?"

"No, sir. I haven't."

"But you did make a print of it?"

"Yes, sir. I did."

220

"And what did it show?"

"It showed Burt Strague walking along the trail."

"Did it show his face plainly?"

"Yes, sir."

"Was it turned toward the camera, or away from it?"

"Toward the camera."

"Was he walking rapidly?"

"He was walking right along, yes, sir."

"Did the background show plainly?"

"No, sir. There is little or no background in any of my shots. I purposely select camera locations in places where a low-power flashbulb and a wide open lens will give me a picture of the animal against a black backdrop."

"What lens is on the camera with which this picture was taken, Mr. Beaton?"

"You wish a technical description?"

"Yes."

"On this particular camera it is a Taylor-Hobson-Cooke anastigmat of six-and-one-quarter-inch focal length, having a speed of F 3.5."

Mason took from his wallet the carbon paper disk Drake had discovered. "Would you say it was about the diameter of this circle of carbon paper?"

Beaton became quite excited. "May I ask where you got that?"

Mason smiled. "Please answer my question first."

"Yes. I would say it was about that—"

Hamilton Burger arose with ponderous dignity, said, "Your Honor, I have hesitated to object, because I felt that I wanted the defendants to have all the latitude possible. I realize that argument on an objection takes up more time than permitting irrelevant questions to be asked and answered. However, if this line of examination is going to continue, I shall certainly object—"

"Just a few more questions, and I am finished," Mason said.

221

Judge Canfield started to say something, then checked himself, muttered curtly, "Very well, Mr. Mason, proceed."

"Now then, as an expert tracker," Mason said, "did you have occasion to examine Burt Strague's tracks in the trail?"

"Yes, I noticed them."

"And did they indicate anything concerning the speed at which he was walking?"

"Really, Your Honor, I *must* object to this," Hamilton Burger said. "This is purely irrelevant. It is not proper cross-examination."

"I can assure the Court it is very pertinent," Mason said. "It tests the recollection of the witness, and it is proper cross-examination as to his qualifications. The Court will remember that the prosecution sought to qualify this witness as an expert on guns and tracks."

Judge Canfield said, "The objection will be overruled. It's proper cross-examination as to the qualifications of the witness as an expert tracker. The witness will answer the question."

"The tracks were spaced rather far apart, and showed he was moving right along," Beaton said.

"And the tracks were regularly spaced?"

"Yes."

Mason smiled at the witness. "And did you notice anything unusual about that, Mr. Beaton?"

"What do you mean?"

"About the fact they were regularly spaced?"

"Why no."

Mason said, "In other words, Mr. Beaton, as an expert tracker, when you see the tracks of a human being walking along a trail, going through a trap which trips a camera shutter, and at the same time suddenly explodes a brilliant flashbulb, you'd naturally expect these tracks to show the man had jumped back, or to one side, wouldn't you? You'd hardly expect to find his tracks moving regularly along at evenly spaced intervals, would you?" Sheer incredulous surprise twisted the muscles of Rodney Beaton's face.

"Can't you answer that?" Mason asked.

"Good Heavens!" Beaton exclaimed. "I never thought of *that!*"

"As an expert tracker, you've noticed what happens with wild animals when they set off a flashbulb, haven't you?"

"Yes, of course. It's—I can't understand it, Mr. Mason."

"But you're certain about the tracks?"

"Yes, sir. I'm certain. I noticed them particularly, although the significance of what I noticed didn't occur to me until just now."

"Exactly," Mason said. "I'll ask you one more question and I am finished. The nature of those photographic traps which you rig up is such that when any strain is put upon a black silk thread stretched across the trail, the picture is taken?"

"Yes, sir."

"And one final question," Mason said. "Wouldn't it be possible for a man to set an alarm clock to the tripping mechanism of your shutter, take a picture at any predetermined time? In other words, at any time the alarm should go off?"

Both Hamilton Burger and McNair were on their feet, both objecting at once. Judge Canfield heard their objections with a frosty smile, said calmly, "Objection overruled. Answer the question."

Beaton, seeming somewhat dazed, said, "Yes, sir. It could be done."

Mason said, "I think that's all, Mr. Beaton. . . . Oh, by the way, I believe the time you noted for the taking of the picture of Burton Strague was at approximately the same time the house of Jack Hardisty in Roxbury was being burglarized, and the night watchman, George Crane, was slugged?"

"I . . . I believe it was. I hadn't, of course, thought of it in that connection before."

Mason bowed with exaggerated courtesy to the two prosecuting attorneys who sat staring, open-mouthed, at the witness. "Have you gentlemen any questions on redirect examination?" he asked.

Burger semed as one in a daze. He turned his eyes from the witness to Mason, then leaned forward to indulge in a whispered conference with McNair.

"Your Honor," Hamilton Burger said, after a few moments, "this is a *most* remarkable development. It not only puts a completely new interpretation upon much of the evidence in this case, but it opens up possibilities that—if the Court please, we'd like an adjournment until tomorrow morning."

"No objection," Mason said.

"Granted," Judge Canfield snapped.

29

Back in his office, Mason opened a drawer in his desk, took out a bottle of rare old cognac, three large snifter glasses, said to Paul Drake and Della Street, "Well, now we can relax. At last I've got that damn clock off of my mind."

"I don't get it," Drake said.

Mason laughed. "Suppose, Paul, we had found an

alarm clock buried in the ground near a point where a man intended to plant a camera to take nocturnal pictures. Suppose we'd further found that one of the persons in the case relied upon a picture taken at night to establish an alibi. What would we have thought?"

Drake said, "Well, of course, if you put it *that* way."

"That's the only way to put it," Mason said. "Those are the simple facts. Too many times we overlook the simple facts in order to consider a lot of extraneous complications which merely confuse the issue. I was responsible for it, Paul. It should be a lesson to me. I tried to work in a lot of stuff about sidereal time in order to get the district attorney of Kern County interested. Naturally, that stuff got into the newspapers, and naturally the murderer read all about it. Therefore, when he got ready to let me discover the clock, it was only natural he would set it on sidereal time."

"But why would he want you to discover it?"

"Because I had started confusing the issues and he thought it would be a good thing to confuse them still more."

"Just what do you think happened?" Della asked.

Mason said, "I can't give you all the details, but I could make a pretty good guess. Vincent Blane had a magazine article lying around his house about how scopolamine would make witnesses talk, confessing crimes which they were really trying to conceal. Naturally, Vincent Blane read it; Martha Stevens, his housekeeper, read it; Adele Blane read it, and Milicent Hardisty read it. Probably all of them thought of that article when it became known that Jack Hardisty had embezzled another ninety thousand dollars and hidden it. . . . Martha Stevens got her boy friend, went so far as to make a practical test. Martha got Milicent Hardisty to procure the drug for her, and then surreptitiously borrowed Milicent Hardisty's gun. Remem-

225

ber, Martha learned of the second embezzlement from overhearing Blane's telephone conversation.

"Milicent didn't learn about the ninety thousand embezzlement until the day of the murder. When she found it out, she was furious. She obviously knew her husband was going to the cabin, and decided on a showdown. She couldn't find her own gun, but her father had a gun that was in the house. She picked it up and started up to the cabin. That, however, was *after* Martha and Smiley had gone to the cabin. She parked her car near the turn-off to the cabin and then became hysterical, and the very force of the nervous storm served to calm her and give her a sane perspective on what she was about to do. She went back and threw the gun away, met Adele, started back to the house. Dr. Macon picked her up in Kenvale. She told him about what had happened. Macon wanted her to go back to the cabin, either to remove some evidence indicating she had been there, to find the gun she had thrown away, or because he didn't entirely believe her story and wanted to check up on what had happened. . . . They got to the cabin well after dark, unwittingly passing Martha and Smiley in the dark on the road, found Jack Hardisty dying. Milicent said she knew nothing about it. You can hardly blame Dr. Macon if he didn't believe her."

"But who killed him?" Della Street asked.

"Martha Stevens gave him a hypodermic of scopolamine," Mason said. "When Jack told them about hiding the money in the tunnel, he wasn't faking. He was telling them the simple truth. They went up to the tunnel, and the money wasn't there. That means someone must have beaten them to it. That person must have removed the money almost as soon as Hardisty had buried it, and then gone on down to the cabin. We can reconstruct what happened then. He found Jack Hardisty drugged and talkative, telling the absolute truth under the influence of

226

the drug. He found the car in which Martha and Smiley had driven up, and of course, Hardisty's car was there also. Hardisty's glasses were broken. He was probably sitting on that big rock outcropping, and the gun which Martha had surreptitiously taken from Milicent Hardisty was lying there on the pine needles where Smiley had thrown it when he hit Hardisty.

"Now this newcomer must have been a friend of Hardisty's; more than a friend—a partner, an accomplice. And he must have been planning to kill Hardisty for some time."

"How do you know that?" Della asked.

"The evidence shows it. When he'd planted that alarm clock the first time, he intended to use it to manufacture an alibi. But he didn't use it because that day Beaton didn't put the camera in that location, and, instead of staying to watch the cameras that night, he took Myrna Payson to a movie."

"But why would this partner want to kill Hardisty?"

Mason smiled. "Put yourself in his place. Hardisty had got caught. Hardisty was going to jail. He was Hardisty's accomplice—and if he had Hardisty out of the way, he'd not only seal his lips but be ninety thousand to the good with no one ever suspecting. . . . The first embezzlement had been a scant ten thousand. That represented money they'd 'borrowed,' probably to finance a mining venture or horse races or stock gambling. The ninety thousand embezzlement was an attempt at blackmail, and it didn't work.

"Put yourself in Burt Strague's position. Jack Hardisty was going to the penitentiary. If Jack talked, Burt Strague would also go up as an accessory. He had intended to make away with Hardisty if he could do so safely. That's why he first planted the alarm clock where he expected Rodney Beaton was going to set up one of his cameras. He was arranging in advance to give himself an alibi. . . .

He came on Jack Hardisty, drugged. Jack Hardisty probably told him he had left some incriminating evidence in that writing desk, evidence that showed the original embezzlement had gone into a joint venture with Burt Strague. And he also told Strague that Martha Stevens had drugged him and that he'd told them where he'd left the money, that he was tired of it all, that he didn't have the nerve to go through with it. When Martha and her boy friend returned from the tunnel, Hardisty was going to tell them everything."

"Where was Milicent all this time?" Drake asked.

"At that particular moment she was probably just parking her car at the turnoff, and starting to walk to the cabin. However, she never did get there. She had hysterics, went back to the road, threw the gun she'd taken with her—her father's gun—away. She then met Adele, went back as far as Kenvale, met Dr. Macon, talked with him and finally returned to the cabin at Dr. Macon's suggestion. Probably Macon wanted to find that gun—and he may have doubted if Milicent's recollection of what had happened while she was hysterical was entirely accurate.

"When he arrived he found Hardisty in bed, dying from a gunshot wound. He naturally assumed Milicent, in her hysteria, had gone a lot farther than she remembered, and that a merciful amnesia had blanked the worst part of what had happened from her mind. That frequently happens in hysteria. In fact *Legal Medicine and Toxicology* by those three eminent authorities, Gonzales, Vance and Helpern, mentions hysteria as an authentic cause of amnesia. So you can begin to see Dr. Macon's position. He felt certain the woman he loved had killed her husband, probably in self-defense, had become hysterical and the hysteria had erased the memory from her mind.

"But to get back to Burt Strague and Hardisty. There

228

was an argument. Hardisty blurted out some things he shouldn't have said. Burt Strague shot him, probably in a struggle. Then, alarmed, he got the wounded man up to the cabin and into bed. He realized Hardisty was dying. He knew that the mud on Hardisty's shoes would show that he'd been to the tunnel. Naturally, he cleaned the shoes, because Burt had removed the money buried there in the tunnel almost as soon as Hardisty had driven away, and he wanted Martha and Smiley to think Hardisty had lied about the tunnel.

"Burt Strague knew that Martha Stevens and her boy friend would very shortly return from their fruitless search of the tunnel. He jumped in Hardisty's automobile, drove it down the grade and off over the embankment. That got rid of the automobile. . . . He didn't have a chance to dispose of some of the other evidence, as he would have liked to. Not until the next morning did he get a chance to dig up his clock—and he had to burglarize the writing desk in the Hardisty residence. That was a ticklish job. When it came to doing it, he relied on the alibi he had already cooked up."

"But how could he have left his picture in the camera," Della Street asked, "if he wasn't actually there?"

"Very easily," Mason said. "With his own camera, he took a flashlight picture of himself walking along the trail. He kept that undeveloped negative in reserve. When Rodney Beaton set up his camera, which was probably right after dark, Burt, taking care to avoid tripping the string which would release the shutter, went up and left tracks in the trail. Then he unscrewed the first element of the lens, inserted the carbon paper disk, replaced the lens, and substituted his exposed film for the one that was in that camera. Remember that it was dark by this time, and he could work by a sense of touch without needing a darkroom. He buried his alarm clock, adjusted the mechanism so it would trip the string and shoot off the

229

flashbulb at the proper time, and then beat it for Roxbury. Remember his slender build. He dressed himself in his sister's clothes, slugged the guard, broke open the desk, got what he was after, returned to the mountains, removed the carbon paper disk from the lens, then went to the Blane cabin, and told the story of having searched all over for Rodney Beaton and his sister. . . . Those are the high points. You can fill in the details."

"But why was the clock twenty-five minutes slow when it was first found?" Drake asked.

Mason grinned. "Because, in order to make the thing work right, Burt Strague wanted to have his alarm clock synchronized with Rodney Beaton's watch, and Rodney Beaton's watch was notoriously inaccurate, so Burt made an excuse to get the time from Beaton and then set his own watch accordingly, and subsequently set the alarm clock according to that time. . . . Once the clock was discovered, we might have tumbled to what it was all about if it hadn't been for the fact that I, myself, mixed the case up by injecting this angle of sidereal time. Having done this to fool the police and the district attorneys of Kern and Los Angeles Counties, I then proceeded to get fooled by it myself, because the murderer promptly picked up my idea and adopted it as his own. . . . And now, we're going to quit talking about the case and have a drink of good old brandy."

"What will they do?" Della Street asked.

"They'll figure the thing out, give Burt Strague the third-degree, and probably get a confession," Mason said. "Strague is something of a weakling, an introvert —the type that is emotional. He won't be a hard nut to crack. I feel sorry for his sister, though. She couldn't have known anything about it, and she's a nice kid. . . . Well, here's to crime."

The door from the outer office opened. Gertie said,

"Mr. Vincent Blane is here. He says he must see you at once."

"Show him in," Mason said.

As Vincent Blane entered the office, Mason took another glass from the drawer of his desk.

"You're just in time," Mason said.

Blane was so excited he could hardly talk. "He confessed," he said. "They got him. He told them all about it, and where he hid the ninety thousand he hijacked from the mine—and about planting that picture. It was an alibi so he could get into Jack's home and—"

Mason said, "I'm sorry, Mr. Blane, we just finished a post-mortem on the case, and decided we weren't going to talk about it until we'd had one good drink."

Vincent Blane seemed somewhat annoyed for a moment, then he grinned and dropped wearily into the big overstuffed leather chair. "At times, Mr. Mason," he said, "you get some remarkably fine ideas. If there's enough of that stuff in the bottle, let's make it *two* good drinks."

Revised U.S. Edition of the Official

Royal Canadian Air Force
Exercise Plans For Physical Fitness

Two books in one / Two famous basic plans

XBX | 12-MINUTE-A-DAY PLAN FOR WOMEN   5BX | 11-MINUTE-A-DAY PLAN FOR MEN

10009/$1.00

GREEN BERET FITNESS PROGRAM

SPECIAL FORCES
6-12 EXERCISE PLAN
COMBATIVES
GUERRILLA EXERCISES

3 graduated exercise plans adapted for everyone

10596/$1.00

75522   E (C) 3/9